THE DOWNFALL OF A BELLYDANCER

Bellydancing and Beyond Book 2

KERRIE NOOR

CONTENTS

NEFERTITI'S GLOSSARY

Roughcast- in Lochgilphead it is considered traditional to cover a new building with grey cement and pebble surface so rough you can, according to the Bag Lady, skin a potato with it.

Cheb Mami's - Algerian singer whose song **Meli Meli,** inspired Neff to create her first dance for others rather than herself.

Oot & aboot - Scottish for out and about a term rarely used in the Highlands due to the weather.

Motorhead - a '70's band that requires head-banging to enjoy.

Zimmer - Named after Mr Zimmer, a man who spent his days walking around the supermarket wheeling an empty trolley. Now used by the elderly in Scotland as weapons of mass destruction for queue jumping.

Durex - In Britain it is the brand name for a condom; in Australia, it is the brand name for sticky tape. There is a joke there, but I haven't quite figured it out yet. Any suggestions welcome. However for this novel either would do as it is highly unlikely that the Pope would either use a condom or wrap presents for his family.

Hen - An affection term for women in Scotland, unless when spoken by a farmer.

Bollocking & Ballistic - The two B words that are usually used when the loss of temper is far greater than the reason behind it.

'Flower of Scotland' - *A song sung by the Scottish when they want to win...and will continue to sing even when they have lost.*

Thingmies - *Scottish for anything you can't remember the name of.*

Dexy's Midnight Runners *—an eighties band who as far as I know never wore any shoes.*

Travelling stock - *or 'travelling folk', are people whose ancestors lived the life of a gypsy, who offered good luck if their 'palms were crossed with silver,' and often seemed to have a connection with dogs and horses.*

Doing My Head in - *that feeling you get when forced to listen to your neighbour's eighteen–year-olds' music at 3 am while trying to sleep.*

Brae - *Scottish term for steep hill, in Lochgilphead it is the steep walk up to the A&E or hospital for mental health problems. Hence the term, 'he up the brae' usually means he's not only up the hill but in residence for a while.*

Buckie or Buckfast – *A traditional Scottish drink for those who can't afford vodka and Red Bull, but are looking for the same effect.*

Best of Hossam Ramzy- *According to many dancers, he is the god of all Egyptian belly dance music.*

Hafla – *In Arabic means a social gathering or party. In the world of belly dance it is the chance for dancers to meet, dance and impress any family and friends who come; sort of like a school concert for belly dancers.*

Shinty - *Scottish game for people with no fear.*

Banoffee pie - *dessert made with bananas and cream which is not only delicious but one of your five a day.*

The kilt -*The kilt liberates a man; suddenly he is prancing about in public, swinging his hips with a 'hide and seek fashion' about what's underneath. He will dance at weddings, like something out of* Strictly Come Dancing; *and walk like he has an arse worth looking at. The kilt holds a seductive promise, often with a larger than life sporran swaying in the front, suggesting something spectacular! And women love it, even after whisky takes hold and flashing brings the mystery to a close. Women still love it!*

Bannockburn - *a very famous battle; Scotland defeated England. It is also the name of a not so famous Scottish cake.*

Catnip - *Some say dope; others say valium for cats.*

To Cave in or Give in - *Apparently (according to Beryl; or was it Mavis?) a hangover in the sun can do that to a man, something to do with testosterone at 35 degrees.*

Midges - *invisible insects, that come out on a warm summer's evening to bite anyone on the west coast of Scotland. Apparently drinking whisky keeps them away.*

Half cut - *another word for 'three sheets to the wind', inebriated, blootered, drunk*

Spun a yarn - *Story telling while spinning wool.*

Sticky Willy - *sticky, green, vine like plant that sticks like Velcro to your clothes.*

Highland fling - *The fling of a Highland man has nothing to do with sex and more to do with wearing a kilt and it flinging about the place while dancing.*

A Do - *an event that's worth getting your legs waxed for!*

Alfresco dancing – *Dancing outside, no picnic or audience required.*

How's it hangin', hen' - *it has nothing to do with hanging or hens, but is a Scottish way of sexing up a how are you?'.*

Simmet - *Scottish for vest...usually the itchy variety worn by those who remember the War.*

MEET THE GANG

Nefertiti: a belly dancing teacher who, according to her is the *'one and only'*.

Rodger: the love of Nefertiti's life, and mentor.

Mavis: Lochgilphead's Post Mistress, a woman that can add, subtract and lick a stamp all at the same time and, while holding a conversation.

Lumpy: the janitor in the community centre his tool box is legendary.

Sheryl: Nefertiti's pal and most famous belly dancing student.

Kay: the least known belly dancing student.

Shifty: the owner of the Argyll, who liked to think his pub more than just a local boozer.

Martin: owner of the post office who likes to think he is more than a post office owner.

Imogene/Imogen: Nefertiti nemesis -she has no idea.

Chubby: is the local butcher, she runs her father's butcher shop, her homemade sausages are legendary.

Steven: is the sort of man no one notices and until Sheryl noticed him...

Puss: Nefertiti cat who likes to think she's Rodger'.

The Co op Bag lady: newcomer to the area.

Betty: Shifty's mother and so much more.

Beryl: a fortune teller, with a love for leather, whips and reading empty wine glasses.

JUST A THOUGHT

When one door closes another opens, so the saying goes.
When one door closes another slams in your face, so the joke goes.
Nefertiti, however, never waited for the door to open, she barged in-
uninvited...
Until she met the Co-op Bag lady.

PROLOGUE

The time for realising your potential often slips by unnoticed.

"My Rodger is building a shed," I said, but no one was listening; no one even looked at me. They were all engrossed, hell-bent on trying to look like King Tut concubines. Except, of course, for Mavis – she was pulling faces in the mirror like a seventeen-year-old attempting his first shave. She had new false eyelashes and was under the impression that it would take years off a face that had been around the block and back again.

Mavis is the oldest in the Sisterhood, my belly dancing troupe; who, along with the others, was trying on outfits for my latest Sisterhood extravagance, oblivious to the cold and me, their mentor.

"Rodger is erecting something, and it's not making me happy," I shouted.

That shut them up, all three of them. They stopped, looked up, and stared at me like I had taken my bra off and revealed three breasts. No one said anything; we all stared at each other until a finger cymbal rolled from the table and clanged onto the floor. Then it started, the jokes about erecting; just like I knew it would.

My troupe has never needed any encouragement when it came to innuendos.

My troupe – the Sisterhood – has entertained, and shimmied all over the Scottish Highlands with an earthiness that has been talked about in all the local papers. We were women of a certain age, who wore sequins over our curves and glittered up our wrinkles for all to see. Nothing stopped us, no poorly lit photograph in the local paper, or half-asleep pensioner snoring in the back of the row; we danced come rain, hail or shine.

We were women proud of every curve, every shake and every step.

Belly dancing is more than a dance, it is a celebration. It keeps things oiled, lubricated and ready for anything. It is better than any HRT or antidepressant and fabulous when one is... celibate. I mean, no woman is past her sell-by date in belly dancing, even Mavis and her fake eyelashes. And who better to teach, inform and mentor than the great Nefertiti herself – a woman made; no, designed to dance.

As I often say to my girls, "Belly dancing oils the ovaries."

I inspire others, I can tell you!

However, tonight I was beginning to wonder. The girls showed little interest and Lumpy the janitor was standing by the door leaning on his broom, with his usual 'time to close up' stance.

"My Rodger has plans," I said. "They are all laid out in my kitchen, and it has put the kibosh on my pyramid." I stared at the blank faces; "the pyramid for meditating under."

I did detect a smirk from one or two faces and a 'give it a rest' from herself under the fake lashes. Mavis never had much time for meditations or pondering as she liked to call it, in fact none of the girls did. Mavis, along with Sheryl, was one of my most loyal, down to earth students; whose idea of 'sorting things out' was shopping, vodka and a good saucy joke, not necessarily in that order. And Mavis's round apple-like body was a testament to such a philosophy, she often struggled with hip circles, but she never gave up. She thought hip twirling would attract a man. She even talked of visiting Egypt, which was, according to some dodgy 'Over Fifties, Single and Still Shimmying' website, full of men who just loved older women, and Mavis was truly tempted.

"But don't you think he is being selfish, ignoring my desires?" I said, with drama. "I mean, my Rodger, the man that made me the woman I am today, is actually planning to build a shed; a shed where I have sat, for years to ponder the goddess within."

"You've never used the pyramid," Mavis muttered, while rolling her coin belt up into a tight ball. She was unmoved, as were the rest of them as they too began to shove their scarves into bags. The class was coming to an end, signalled by the janitor now in the room and pushing his broom about; Lumpy is a stickler for finishing on time.

"Every man needs a shed," he muttered, as he stopped to pump air freshener into the air. "Why shouldn't your man?" Pearls of wisdom from a janitor whose broom cleaned the floor with as much effect as his lavender spray.

And Lumpy didn't stop there; he went on and on about a man and his castle, and how a drawbridge was more a man's best friend than a dog. "Every man should be able to turn his back on the world,' he said, "A man needs time to think, chew over the day, and put away his armour. He needs a moment to slide on his slippers; with no sharing of the paper, or the remote control."

No wonder Lumpy lives on his own, honestly. I was on the verge of making some sarcastic comment about his 'inability to share a broom let alone push it' when I looked around; they were all agreeing with him, my girls. One whiff of a free drink and you can't see them for dust. I ask you, where is all the support, the comradeship? I'll tell you – out the window as fast as Lumpy's offer of a 'quick drink' in the Argyll.

I left soon after that, and like all great artists sulked all the way home, refusing the after-class tradition of a 'tonic with whatever is on special in the Argyll'. Instead, I went home, scrunched His Nib's shed plans into a ball and tossed them onto the pile of logs drying by the fire.

I had worked my underwire off for that troupe and no one seemed aware of it. For months we had been practicing dancing with canes. I thought it would instil a new dynamism into the trio. It could maybe even encourage past students to return.

A cane dance means moving your hips with authority. A dancer twirls her cane around with military panache, with an attitude that declares 'up yours' to anyone who says belly dance is for wimps. The idea is to twirl one cane (or two like me, if you are a master) while dancing on your knees, performing back bends and even a little balancing on your head. I had the old folks at the Fyne Home spellbound and it took a full song before the usual ones fell asleep. The staff were so impressed that even after the accident with the tea trolley they asked me to come back.

Rodger said that I hypnotised them with my cane twirling and I knew the group could do the same. I had planned a group dance with a solo for Sheryl in one verse, a duet for Kay and Mavis in another verse and me doing a final dynamic piece with two canes, but their lack of enthusiasm confused me. I finally gave Mavis the chance to perform at the front and she hardly batted an eye, let alone issued a, "Cheers, Neff. I can't wait to do my bit for the Sisterhood."

"It's our greatest extravagance yet," I said. "A performance like no other we have done and I have just the right music." No one said a word.

I stood in my kitchen with only the drip of the kitchen tap to break the silence. "Bugger the lot of you" I shouted, and tossed my bag of costumes onto the table. A loud clatter followed as coin belts and zills spilled out onto the table and the floor. Puss, Rodger's cat, looked up from her basket and meowed.

"And you can wait as well!" I shouted. She meowed again and then got up and wrapped herself around my legs. It was a pathetic ploy to win me around, and it worked.

Feeding her is usually Rodger's job but as he was nowhere to be seen and Puss would not give up the 'leg hugging,' I gave in and opened a tin of cat food. Puss took one whiff and was off through the cat flap and into the night, while I was left clutching a half emptied can, with its mid-Atlantic fish aroma now filling the kitchen.

My life, it seemed, was full of turncoats.

Chapter One

A FALLING STAR

Never judge a dance by its audience.

The day I first heard the Egyptian drums I knew I had found my calling: to liberate women from a fear of their bodies and entertain the world. And it was Rodger who made it imaginable, it was he who understood, and he who called me, 'Queen of the Clyde', 'Loch Fyne's finest', and finally his 'Nefertiti'.

"No one dances like you," he said, "and I intend to show the world." *Well, at least Argyll,* and I believed him.

In the past Rodger had been my rock, the foundation of my artistic journey; a man who understood my talents and the need to express them. Who, back in the days when I first moved to Argyll, recognised that I was a performer of great status, and had star quality as he called it.

I was Mid Argyll's only Middle Eastern dancer whose legendary shimmies and entrances were talked about days after a performance, who had been mentioned in the local paper more times than the traffic warden or the local councillor, and I loved it, because my whole body was made for performing.

And Rodger was always there for me, through all my performances – keeping the old folk quiet, stopping them from falling asleep and turning up the music when the crowd grew noisy. He would even defend me, in public, to people who were very vocal in their disapproval. Those who were often under the impression (and made it known) that belly dancing was stripping and way beyond the realms of a 'menopausal housewife'.

"She's no housewife," he used to say. "We're not even married."

Between you and me, the Sisterhood owes much to Rodger and his ability to master any situation. He took care of all our staging and what he could do with a few solar power torches, and a mobile download was pure genius.

Which was why I found his building of a shed over my meditation space so disturbing; and Lumpy's 'drawbridge, slippers' speech didn't help either. I mean my Rodger has never owned a pair of slippers in his life, he prefers the feel of shag pile between his toes.

Lumpy, the all-seeing, all-knowing janitor, has manned the community centre, for as long as I have been in Lochgilphead, and is, to quote Mavis, part of the bricks and roughcast. What would he know about Rodger and his footwear? Just because he has his portrait hanging up on the *Wall of Gratitude* – that's the foyer, to you and me – doesn't make him any more than what he is: a janitor who has been there since time began, with a nickname of unknown origin.

God knows how long that photo has been there, hanging as Kay says, "like yesterday's washing." But there it hangs right beside Sheila, Lochgilphead's first yoga teacher and vegetarian, who brought the humble turnip into the twentieth century, *with a little cinnamon* and introduced the WRI to 'mindful' baking.

That photo is a sad reminder of a young Lumpy flashing a full set of teeth, a poor man's Elvis in overalls. I mean, I have loads of pictures of me when I was young, when I could spellbind more than just the old and infirm. But as I said to my Rodger: "Who would want a picture of their glory years hung on the *Wall of Gratitude* for members of the Young Farmers' Association to smirk at?"

Time is never kind. Look at Lumpy... No longer the young man with a full head of hair, he now loiters about the entrance of the community centre with a haunted look. A skinny man who gave up smoking the day he gave up wearing his council overalls in protest about the council cuts, and no one noticed.

An hour after the 'turncoat' belly dancing class, I hadn't moved. I was rooted to the kitchen stool staring at Puss's untouched food wondering who would come home first, when Rodger stumbled through the door. He too had been at the Argyll, his newfound haunt. I told him about Lumpy's 'slipper philosophy' and Rodger said little. In fact so engrossed was he in balancing a few cat biscuits on top of Puss's mid-Atlantic cat food that I began to wonder if he had noticed me at all.

"Every week he stands there," I said, "watching me squirm at the empty page of signatures for my class ... right beside the two pages of names for the Zumba class."

Rodger looked at me with a flat expression. "I am sure he doesn't watch."

"And I hadn't even removed my coin belt let alone turned off Hossam Ramzy and there he was sweeping the floor like I had already left ... It's hard not to take it to heart."

"Swings and roundabouts," said Rodger, "one day wobbling flesh will return, and you will be at the top of the pile." Which I must admit had me wondering; Rodger could be, as Sheryl likes to put it, cryptic at times.

I wanted to say more, I wanted Rodger's shoulder to lean on, his listening ear. I wanted to talk about the Gala day; and Rodger's ideas for the sound system.

"I had found the best music ever," I said: "Cheb Mami's *Meli Meli,* and it's perfect for a small group with solo dances."

"What?"

"For the Gala day."

He looked, tired and irritable; apparently building a shed can do that to a man, especially after a few at the Argyll.

"It just that I have this idea for bagpipes with canes..."

Rodger let out a sigh.

"And I'll finish with that dance I did at the rugby union 'do' – you know how they loved it. Two canes and some tilts..."

"They were out of it," he said, "drunk, and looking for more than a few tilts, we had to cut short the dance, remember?"

"No... Was it not a power cut?"

And then he looked at me. "There's only three left in the class. Can you not take a hint?"

Hint? What the hell was he talking about?

Chapter Two

THE TURN COAT

Use your exits well; sometimes it is all you have.

*L*ochgilphead is not the sort of place that attracts visitors; in fact, there are usually only two reasons why anyone visits Lochgilphead – to spend time with relatives and gloat, or because they were offered a job, and didn't investigate before they accepted. Lochgilphead has a Co-op, a newsagent's, a couple of coffee shops, several pubs, and Rodger's bookshop called *The Read and be Thankful*.

A name inspired by *The Rest and be Thankful*, a remote place at the end of a remote road through Glen Coe in Scotland; a place where, in the past, travellers on horseback or in a carriage would stop and look at the view to- 'rest and be thankful'; and a place where we stayed in a camper van on our first night together and truly did, at times, rest and be thankful...

This morning, however, I was feeling uneasy. It had been two weeks since Rodger's cryptic hint comments and he had been unusually quiet. He said that he was engrossed in the shed preparations, which I found hard to believe. I mean the shed had arrived in a flat pack, and was whisked up as quickly as a three-man tent by him, Shifty (his new best pal) and Sheryl's husband Steven. But Rodger was obsessed and now suddenly he had better things to do and all of it in the shed.

The new, quiet, Rodger had me stumped I had no idea what to do next except make another coffee and stir it. I watched Rodger walk into the kitchen with a grunt and little eye contact. I slid an espresso his way.

"Rodger," I said. "Lumpy reckons I should try Zumba."

He pulled a croissant from the fridge and placed it in the microwave. "Why would he say that?"

"He says folk are bored and that's why they don't come anymore."

"Profound for a janitor," he said, searching for a plate.

"Mavis says that folk are bored of my classes." I looked at him for a moment, in his usual shed attire. "Are you?" I asked. "Bored with me...my...dancing?"

"What?" He was now scraping small flecks of butter onto his croissant. A few months ago it would have been a slab of the stuff and at least two croissants; now it seems he's watching his waistline along with having a new secret life in the shed.

"The Gala day, you're not interested like you used to be, it's like you don't care."

He looked at me with a sigh. "Is ten years not enough?" And, before I could answer or offer him some homemade jam for the croissant, he was off into the garden with a throwaway comment: "Shifty's visiting later."

I stood at the kitchen window and looked into the garden. Puss slipped out of the cat flap and followed her hero. I stared at Rodger's back as he bent to pat her; she looked up and purred, and then followed as he disappeared behind the hydrangeas by the shed. And I wondered how long it had been since he had let me kiss his back, his neck or any other part of his body, for that matter.

After two more espressos and a flapjack laughingly called delicious, I headed out to the post office. I wanted to see Mavis to ask her why she hadn't been to the last couple of classes since her flippant remark about my pyramid and of course I wanted some sympathy.

Mavis was my first student, my first pal when I moved here, and nothing gets past her. She was the one who told everyone how fabulous belly dancing was; she advertised, she talked and she proclaimed. Not only in the Stables coffee shop where they turn a blind eye to her slipping whisky in her coffee, but in her newly acquired post office job. Of course that job is perfect for her; working behind the post office counter means she can find out anything and everything. She could actually make the *Fyne News* sellable with her knowledge of the town.

I dumped my Amazon returns on the counter and started to tell Mavis about how my Rodger wasn't like my Rodger anymore and how 'between you and me' I was worried.

Mavis looked at me over the counter. "I'm working," she said, "and it's hardly between you and me in the post office, is it?" Mavis has one of those faces that could do with a little waxing, and lipstick that never quite obeys the line of her lips. And that day, I noticed that her lips were highlighted by fine beads of perspiration. I wondered what was up.

"But there's no one here," I said, gesturing to the shop that was empty apart from a solitary pensioner staring at the envelope selection. Mavis sighed.

"Rodger says it is his artistic temperament, which is funny because he hasn't painted since his Flower of Scotland Exhibition. And he has started flouncing – I thought that was my role!" Mavis looked over the top of her glasses. "Is that what you call it?"

And then I began to tell her about his latest episode. "It was particularly brutal," I said, "as it was more Puss's fault than mine, although Rodger didn't see it that way." Puss had used the scrunched-up plans for the shed as cat litter. Apparently it was easier for Puss to catapult into the log pile and foot-pedal rough paper into some sort of pliable cat litter material, than saunter through a large cat flap and use the recently weeded garden. For some reason, Rodger seemed to think it was my fault, with a 'you put her up to it' sermon.

"It's like he is trying to pick a fight," I said, "over anything."

"Hmmm"

"Why would he do that?"

Mavis said nothing; her gold-ringed fingers were flashing across the computerised till with irritating speed. She could, at times, be annoyingly absorbed. I've seen her serve four customers, down a coffee and a roll and sausage all at the same time. "If he just saw me dance again, then I'm sure things would pick up," I said to her.

"You should try Zumba," she said, while shuffling a few papers.

I stared at her. "Zumba? Me try Zumba? Why?" I wanted to tell her how much I hated Zumba I wanted to shout *Zumba makes me want to spit*, but I didn't, Mavis thought the teacher was a wonderful human being.

"Zumba," said Mavis, "is the new yoga, and everyone is doing it."

What she means by everyone, is everyone from my class!

"Zumba is a poor imitation of dance," I said, and was just about to explain why when Imogen, (formerly known as Imogene) walked in.

Imogen, Lochgilphead's resident calligrapher has ditched calligraphy for Zumba, and now teaches. And to celebrate her new artistic direction she had changed her name, (apparently it looked better on posters).

The pensioner looked up from the envelope section, as Imogen picked up the *Glasgow Herald* and walked over to the counter to pay for it; like it was the height of intelligence to read the *Glasgow Herald*. I was just about to make some sarcastic reference about being a *Record* woman myself when I heard the Stick Insect, as I liked to call her, say to Mavis, "are you going to Zumba this week because I could do with another for the troupe? We're going to start filming!"

"Mavis," I said, ignoring the reference to filming – it was probably just a mobile upload for YouTube. "You go to Zumba?"

Mavis said nothing, but stared at her till.

"You go to Zumba?"

"Absolutely," said Imogen. "My Mavis is a star."

I looked from Imogen's pristine pert eyebrows to Mavis, the beaded sweat on her upper lip now almost dripping. How could she?

My Mavis had gone to the other side with not one ounce of shame. She was no longer my Mavis... she was now a star for the opposition. If she had gone to Russian classes or joined a gym, I would understand; if she had dropped me for mountain climbing or rowing a boat, I could live with that. But her leaving me for Zumba, the very reason my own classes were dying... How could she?

Mavis looked red and flustered.

"Zumba won't work your bits and pieces," I muttered. "And you won't be able to cough freely when you are old..."

Mavis said nothing but I caught a look between her and the 'wonderful human being'.

"I mean we all want to age with ...reassurance," I said.

Mavis leant forward, "No one wants to hear about coughing when you're old," she said.

"I do," said the pensioner, clutching a packet of cost cutter envelopes. She turned to a woman entering the shop with a questioning look. "What I'd give for a decent laugh with no ...worries."

The younger woman looked back, confused. "I only came in for a top up."

Mavis told me to move away from the counter, "Please don't start with your *belly dance cure-all* speech," she said. "It's bad enough in your class. It is one of the reasons why I left. You talk too much about things no one wants to hear...You're just too blunt for your own good."

I looked at the pensioner, who had now moved onto the Scottish section and was turning a Scotland the Brave mug in her hand like she had never seen one before, I decided to leave, or should I say retreat; then Imogen stopped me. She fluttered her false nails across the top of my arm like we were best buddies.

"Dance is not all about the pelvis," she said. "Ask Mavis."

Chapter Three

ZUMBA

When in doubt strut, and don't stop until you are out of sight.

My Rodger was beginning to make me feel unwanted; it seemed as if he had cut himself off and become unreachable.

Rodger said it was nothing to do with me... when I say he said nothing, I mean, when I ask 'is it me?' he said nothing. Rodger instead talked about his shed, went off to his shed, and when he wasn't in the shed, spent time buying things for his shed. And if you saw the shed, you would wonder what all the fuss was about.

As I said to my girls, "I think we are going through the seven year itch, three years late; and I blame Shifty." Six months ago Rodger took up assertiveness classes, and ever since then he has been a changed man who picked over everything and was too busy for my belly dancing nonsense, as he had taken to calling it. And it was Shifty who ran the class that convinced him to come.

Sheryl said the last thing an assertiveness class would teach is to pick, and Kay agreed, stating that Rodger and I were just going through a low patch, or dip as Sheryl called it, and would soon come out of it.

But I felt I was going through more than a patch and I had no idea how to change things. Rodger had started to belittle my belly dancing, the man so passionate about my dance that he called me Nefertiti?

That night as I walked into the community centre for my class, I felt low. I could hear the Zumba music blasting through the whole centre and I could hear her - Imogen goading everyone on like some sort of dancing guru with amazing pronunciation.

"Wonderful darlings."

The belly dancing page was blank with not one single signature; I knew after today that Mavis would not turn up, but Kay? Sheryl? Sheryl had mumbled something about her hubby wanting a night in, or perhaps something to do with the in-laws, but I hadn't been listening. Now, as I stared at the blank pages, I wished I had.

I kidded on I didn't care. I put on my best brave face and stood at the entrance waiting for a smirk from Lumpy's thin lips-bracing myself for his usual sarcasm.

Do your worst, Elvis. I thought and he looked back with a smile of sympathy...he never usually smiled at me. What was up with him? Then I noticed he had on a pair of overalls that were not only clean but had been ironed. The only other time Lochgilphead had seen such a sight was the grand opening of the *Wall of Gratitude* years ago. The red tape was cut by some *Britain's Got Talent* contestant who could make her dog perform to *Bolero*, and Lumpy, in his finely pressed overalls, was there to provide the scissors. Now here he was after all these years, turned out like a new handkerchief, being kind to me. I was truly thrown...

"You were made for Zumba, Mavis, and don't let anyone else tell you different," shouted Imogen from the Zumba class.

"We all have our dips, love," he muttered.

Lumpy had never called me anything before, let alone love, usually he just stood and watched me sign with the blank uninterested face of a thirteen-year-old. This time he actually looked human, and as the stinking Zumba music filled the whole of the community centre, he closed the book. "It's all a phase," he muttered and talked about a refund for the room.

"I am going to use the room," I said, "I need to prepare for the Gala day." And before Lumpy could protest, utter a *love* or flash me another poor cow smile, I strutted, and continued to strut even when I heard Mavis – my whisky sharing Mavis – cackling over the beats of Zumba. I was going to dance until I felt good again I was going to dig deep and find my inner goddess and an empty class was not going to get in my way.

As I walked into the empty room, I could hear Imogen's posh drawl through the wall like some well-oiled royalty.. She was talking about Chubby, the local butcher, doing a piece about the Zumba premier in the *Oot and Aboot* section of the *Loch Fyne News*. Chubby is the local butcher, who sees herself as a woman of wit and intelligence and so much more than a butcher. She writes for the newspaper. And now, apparently, she loves Zumba as much as she used to love my belly dancing.

At one time, the Sisterhood performances were one of Chubby's favourite topics to write about. We were women not to be messed with, she wrote, an inspiration of *glittering, coin belts* with *the scariest war cry she had ever heard,* who had reached *a pinnacle, the crest of a hip-popping wave* that even she had never imagined.

Not now. She has turned, and recently written that I, Nefertiti, have to accept that *the baton has been passed and the pinnacle has been toppled; chopped down and stamped on.* According to her, the world wants their women young, half my age; women like Imogen, who are as thin as an empty crisp packet.

I haven't bought a Chubby's sausage since.

I had already decided to play some Native American chant music; it was bold, rhythmic and would definitely drown out the Zumba shit from next door. Dancing can be so exhilarating especially when you performing to a new song, it's like sex with a new partner – you're never quite sure what you are going to do next, but hopefully whatever you do works and if you're lucky you'll remember- really lucky you'll get to do it again.

I tell my girls that an empty space is like a blank canvas, "use your instincts- set the scene, walk the room like a queen and own it. Let the audience get a good look at your costume, stretch your spine; fill your lungs with music and expand your rib cage. Your body will look amazing and then, when you are ready, stretch out your arms and invite the audience in."

Or, as in my case, strut and pretend.

As the drums started, I began. I lifted my veil into the air with a 'stuff you' to the class next door and took in a deep breath. I was going to dance my heart out, fill the room and forget.

I posed and *with the vision of a captive audience* let my arms paint the story, starting with the hands. Chunky fingers look amazing when in tune with a violin, even mine and for a moment I watched them *do their thing* before the movement traced up my arms and finally into a shoulder roll. I then twirled my scarf around my head and as the pace of music increased, circled the room, my feet following the melody and my hips moving to the drumbeat- followed by my favourite- hip drops and shoulder shimmies, soon the beat and my body were one, connecting deeper to the music.

Belly dancing is all about moving different parts of the body to different parts of the music. I like to think of it as painting the music with my body, and as I twirled to the chants of Native Americans I almost forgot everything.

It was only short piece, and as it came to a close I circled my hips, faster as I spun around the room. I followed with a head twirl, circling my hair like a Motorhead fan finishing with -a Middle Eastern call...

"Lah lah lah lah lah Loi!!!"

Lumpy started to knock on the door...

"Lah lah lah lah lah Loi!!!"

He knocked again; I opened my eyes and there he was broom poised; apparently, I was disturbing the Russian reading group across the hall.

A couple of hours later, I was standing in the Argyll's ladies in a cubicle the size of a kennel with a genital hygiene poster stuck on the door. "Don't soap," it said, with *Jenny makes it happen* scratched on the top, along with a number twice as long as a mobile number should be. I had often stared at that poster and wondered how much the graffiti artist had had to drink to leave such a useless number, but not tonight. Tonight the numbers were blurring in and out of focus, like an eye test with the wrong set of glasses on.

I was trying to centre myself, regroup, but nothing was happening.

I had been in the Argyll with Kay and Sheryl- the remains of the Sisterhood – the remains of a group of women who would perform at the drop of a bra strap and I had accepted every drink offered to me.

I had taken pity on myself because I had heard the worse news ever. Zumba had been asked to perform at the Ardrishaig Gala day. Imogen and her skin-tight Lycra would now be entertaining in the car park. For years the Sisterhood had performed at the Gala day, now it seemed they, the committee wanted something new, fresh and innovative. I may as well have taken the canes and shoved them up a drain pipe.

"We will decorate the car park with the biggest poster ever," said Imogen."We'll show Ardrishaig what we got,"

"And give 'em a taste of real dancing," chipped in Mavis.

I heard cheers from the class and wanted to cry and yell at the same time. I wanted to throw a tantrum like a baby or, even better, pull that tight blonde ponytail of Imogen's hard and silence her posh purr.

I crashed my hips yet again against the toilet roll holder, stumbled out of the toilet, turned on the tap and glared at myself in the mirror. Not the best thing to do when under the influence, you are either scowling or smiling like an idiot, with mascara drawing a road map around your eyes. But staring in the mirror is something we women do when times are tough. We stare at our face and curse it, as if every wrinkle and droop is the reason why we feel so lousy, the reason why our world has caved in.

I didn't give a toss about being centered any more. *More 'tonic and whatever' was what I wanted* and I headed back into the bar.

Chapter Four

THE ARGYLL

One is never enough, and three is way too many.

Shifty was standing behind the bar, polishing an endless supply of glasses and staring at Sky Sports. It was Tuesday night; nothing much happened on a Tuesday night. In fact, Shifty only kept the bar open for the dance class women. And tonight I could tell he was regretting it; he had been polishing the same glass for ten minutes.

Shifty runs the Argyll and, according to Sheryl, he runs it like no other. Sheryl swears by him, but she's easily impressed. She thinks because he remembers what she drinks, he is actually interested in what she has to say.

Truth is, Shifty, has little time for women.

He wasn't always like that; in fact, he was even happily married until his wife left him for Ardennes – or the Latin arsehole, as Shifty liked to call him – and Shifty and I developed a friendship. It was the sort of relationship that revolved around the odd free drink from Shifty and me listening. We shared the same dislike for Ardennes.

❄

When I first headed for Scotland, I packed up what was left of my life, dumped it on the back of my moped and drove. I ended up one dark afternoon driving into the quiet main street of Lochgilphead. I stopped and pulled up at the Stables, a coffee shop synonymous with mayonnaise and chips. Mavis, who I only knew back then as the lady with no eye makeup, offered me a hot chocolate.

When she pointed out the new belly dancing teacher, Ardennes, sauntering across the street, I decided to stay. Ardennes was just the sort to make a girl forget her past. Ardennes was the type of man you could never tire of looking at. He made belly dancing look easy and track suit pants like the latest fashion.

Each night we all piled into the community centre, moving into larger rooms as more women joined his class. We learnt so much. He was a man passionate about chilli and spices, a man from the sun and a man who liked to teach with his hands on every woman's hips – except mine. Nothing I did would make him notice me.

I grew my hair long and lost weight; I practiced hard. I stood in the front line and made jokes, stood at the back row and smouldered. I pretended to sprain my ankle. Then I brought a pair of stilettos, wore them to the class and really sprained my ankle. Nothing made him look at me, absolutely nothing.

When his wife ran off leaving little more than an 'I've been miserable and it's your fault' note, Shifty turned to talking and coffee. He transformed himself. He gave up the drink, the fags, and the fatty food, and even took up running for a while. He wanted his wife, but when she didn't come back, he changed. And he seemed pleased when I took up teaching the classes, even told me to "beat that bastard at his own game."

At first he welcomed the new belly dancing class into his pub. Each Tuesday he would arrange for all the dancing girls to have a special half-priced vodka or gin with tonic for the first hour. And then he discovered assertiveness and started to teach it, for men only.

I looked at the streamlined man in front of me, polishing glasses with precision. He lifted up a wine glass, and peered at it in the light.

"Zumba has taken all my gigs," I muttered.

He looked at me. "You need to move on," he polished, "get a grip".

"But we were a celebration of ....womanliness," I said.

"So you say."

"My girls weren't past their sell-by date; they still had something to offer."

"I don't remember anyone saying they were too old, except you," said Shifty, holding the glass to the light again. "You're the only one who talks about 'sell-by dates'. Perhaps that is why they left," he said, finally putting down his glass.

Sometimes I wonder about Shifty. He has changed since the 'bastard in Lycra' days. In fact, he seemed to have little time for belly dancing and was even talking of stopping the happy hour drinks with a 'times are hard' excuse. Sheryl says he's gone upmarket, and is talking of changing the face of the Argyll.

"We had it all," I said.

"What, the women or the girls?"

Ignoring Shifty's sarcasm I carried on, "I should be taken seriously, not tossed aside I mean... I am Nefertiti, a woman whose man swings from her bedroom chandelier."

Shifty pointed his remote at Sky Sports and turned it to the shopping channel.

"I've seen your chandelier," said Shifty. "The only thing that could possibly swing from that is a banana skin." *Shifty had seen my chandelier when; and why?*

"She's tanked up," said Kay. "Let's get her home." I wasn't going anywhere, I had more to say and fuelled by vodka on an empty stomach I was going to say it, even if no one was listening, I didn't care. I was witty, talented and seeing double.

I ranted on about how we had performed everywhere, how everyone loved us, I was on a roll. Until Shifty pointed out that back then our only competition was Scottish country dancing; the sort of dancing that requires a good partner; which as Kay pointed out was not easy to find in a small town like Lochgilphead. Undeterred, I continued...

I reminded them about the showdown at the Carer's Centre, which no one talks about now; an unpleasant affair where there was a double booking. There was an undignified tussle in the toilets, a few finger cymbals were broken and words (unprintable) were said. In the end we were all asked to leave, dropped for bingo of all things.

"And now they too have Zumba, I suppose," said Shifty.

"Exactly," I said.

Sheryl handed me my jacket.

Mavis had arrived in an explosion of earthy colours along with Lumpy, sporting a tartan green shirt and seeing two of them was making me feel a little queasy.

Mavis looked at Lumpy and giggled. And before I had a chance to find out what was so funny I was ushered yet again out the door, with Kay on one side and Sheryl on the other.

Chapter Five

THE HANGOVER

One chocolate is soon forgotten, but the joy of an orgasm can last a whole day.

I met my Rodger ten years ago in Glasgow. I was on my way up north, and he was sitting outside his antiques store. I remember it so well; Glasgow was sunny, a rare moment.

I was on my way home from the Goddess Festival in the Midlands, where I had experienced the pleasures and wisdom of Polynesian massage along with various tribal dances. I was walking down Woodlands Road drinking in the sun and feeling inspired, womanly, and in need of a good seeing to when I came across Rodger sucking on the last of his cigar.

He had a cappuccino on a quaint little table beside him, along with a copy of *Swing with the Old Guys*, an antiques magazine that swung for about three editions. He was wearing green, and his hair came over his eyes. His moustache, which I grew to love as much as the man himself, was firm and almost got in the way of his cigar.

He placed his cup on its saucer, the table wobbling a little, and his eyes never left mine.

"You looking or buying?" he said.

"Depends," I said.

"On what?" he asked.

"On your price! Are you cheap, dear or middle of the road?"

He pulled out a deck of cards and motioned me to play. I hate cards, I hate games, but I played him like a cat with a sparrow, and I let him win; I knew he would want more. And more he did. Rodger, puffed with success, agreed to close his shop early and treat me to a posh bistro just off the Great Western Road.

The bistro was set in a cobbled lane near the underground, with casual decor and French cuisine cooked and served by the owner. Rodger was completely at home ordering in French and even tasted the wine without getting his moustache wet.

"Foam," he whispered, looking at my fish course, "on scallops; a marked improvement on a sauce." I smiled back, I had spent the whole day on rice cakes and dried apricots, so I wasn't about to complain. I watched as he picked up a thin wedge of carrot and bit into it and then offered me the other half. "The more expensive the restaurant, the crunchier the vegetable," he murmured.

He made me blush in those days, something a woman of a certain age should have grown out of. However, a man with a soft voice and stiff moustache was new to me. The men I had known before thought eating out was a fish supper at your local, and foreign food was a kebab served by someone with dark skin. Rodger swept me off my feet with his fancy food, his brown eyes and questions. Back then he liked to talk; he liked to share his thoughts and feelings and was happy to wait for my reply.

Not now. Rodger was as interested in what I had to say as Puss was in a plate of lentils.

I was standing in my front doorway, fumbling for my key. The girls had dropped me off from the Argyll, opened the front door and pushed me in while I was still looking for it.

"You're in now, Neff; you don't need your key. Go to sleep!" *I think that was Kay's voice – she always sounded pissed off after a few...*

I stumbled inside and pushed the door shut with my backside, setting off another stagger. Rodger was asleep on the big white couch we chose together, with Puss curled up in the curve of his legs. He was in the foetal position, which, in our bed, meant his arms were around me with his breath fluttering across my shoulder.

The last time I sat down on the couch to be with him he got up in seconds to feed Puss, and Puss hadn't even meowed.

Puss looked up as I walked by. She purred, I purred back and stumbled upstairs. Rodger was out for the count. Nothing would wake him.

The next morning I woke up with no sign or sound of His Nibs. I had a hangover, and I had forgotten how rubbish it was to have them. I had forgotten what it was like to wake up regretting the night before, with your insides kicking up a storm; with feelings of regret, remorse and a blurred memory of what happened; with knowing somewhere in the back of your mind you had spilled it all in an ugly way that you would never do sober. I guess I am talking about inexplicable shame and a blinding headache.

Of course, having such a hangover is one thing. What makes it worse is having a hangover when your life is not only what you didn't plan, but is more like the life you ran away from and thought *that was that*; *never again*. Now, as I stared at our chandelier suspended above the bed, a sinking feeling of 'here we go again' welled up in my stomach. Swinging from the chandelier was a note, scrunched up but readable from the bed. 'I'll do the shop this morning,' it read in black angry writing, which I had become accustomed to. Ever since the incineration incident, Rodger has taken to leaving curt notes. They are usually on the bathroom mirror, because, according to one of his brief notes, he knows I will always go there.

As I inhaled cat breath, I realised that the worst had happened. Puss, as if to make my hangover that bit worse, was sitting on my stomach, exhaling fumes into my face. The only way out, I thought, was to feed the beast, which meant leaving the bed.

I rolled out of bed like an accident and emergency patient being tipped off a stretcher, pulling Mr Rational's note as I fell. I flopped onto the floor, feebly scrunched up said note, and with great effort, tipped it into the bin.

"All yours, Puss," I muttered, and immediately regretted it.

After Puss was given an anchovies and mackerel delicacy, which had me vowing to join the vegan society, I flopped into the chaise lounge with no care of what I looked like. Instead, I looked out through the patio doors and watched the birds tuck into last night's fish supper.

It was a low moment, what I called a Sheryl moment, so I phoned her.

"I wondered when you'd surface," she said, with not a hint of a smile.

Sheryl and I go back a long way, too long for me to count. She is married to Stephen, a man who works in the local library, and she has no idea what it is like to have an enigma for a partner.

Sheryl, despite her poor taste in clothes, is a woman who can make sense out of a muddle. She reassures and soothes like warm hands on a back and makes the best coffee you could ever imagine. Sheryl always makes coffee in a crisis and, at times like this; she will even use cream, sugar and whisky. She says fat and sugar are nature's best medicine and I was hoping for the same this morning.

She arrived wearing a red outfit and stood at the door. I looked at her. I swear she must have got dressed in a cupboard, well, at least in a room with no mirror. And for a moment my stomach stopped lurching and my hangover was forgotten as I caught sight of a woman wearing what looked to be a giant tartan sock, coordinated in red and green. According to Sheryl, it was all the rage. I had my doubts. And as for ponchos... who wears ponchos?

"Did anyone see you in that?" I said.

Sheryl didn't even smile, let alone laugh and Sheryl always laughs. Since Steven and her got together, laughing has become second nature to Sheryl ; apparently multiple orgasms can do that to a woman...Not that I am jealous. Laughing has never been my best feature- I am more of a smolder-er according to Rodger, like "last night's bonfire."

But this morning Sheryl had about as much mirth as an inpatient waiting for root canal treatment. She moved about my home lost in her own thoughts; it seemed she had little to say. Normally she would be bustling about like a Scottish Mary Poppins, whistling and chatting. But this morning there was no bustling, or whistling. She said nothing, but handed me a black coffee and a thin limp digestive. *I didn't even know we had any in the house.*

I made some jokey comment about Steven doing time in the library and her being at a loose end. She didn't even smile. "Maybe you should lay off the hard stuff for a while," she sighed. "You're getting things all out of proportion."

Once, after a few, she had said to me, "Neff, when you start swearing, I start panicking."

She had been on the whisky at the time, so I was impressed with the literal way in which she expressed herself. In those days Sheryl had no limits and always ended up singing Dolly Parton songs while trying to maintain balance on whatever seat she was perched on.

Now it seemed that I had been doing the perching on a stool and falling off, while telling everyone how much I hated Dolly Parton and Barbara Streisand, which caused Shifty, who loved all musicals, to nearly choke on his diet coke.

"Shifty refused to play any belly dancing music," said Sheryl. "Do you remember?"

"No."

"To be specific, you asked for the cane dance song."

"Cane dance?"

"And then when no one had a clue what you were talking about, you slid off your stool while trying to balance a pint glass on your head. 'Just like Mavis', you said. And that's when Mavis walked in."

"I don't remember that bit."

"Fortunately the glass wasn't full."

"I did wonder about my top."

Sheryl, a reformed drinker, wasn't helping my hangover much; in fact she was making it worse, you'd think feeling sick over the smell of anchovies and mackerel cat food was punishment enough?

"Sheryl," I said. "Did you and Kay not take me home?"

"Finally, after you insulted Mavis."

"What?"

"You said Mavis's ability to wave a scarf was on a par with a man who waves flags at airplanes. Then...went on about how Lycra was for roller skating teenagers, not 'Rail Scot pensioner's card holders'. And then, God forbid, you went on about ..."

"Oh God, don't tell me...the ability to cough freely when you're older!"

Sheryl nodded.

"She left soon after that, didn't even finish her whisky. You did, though."

Well, at least that explains the headache.

Puss pounced on my lap, completed a few needling moves on my chest, and then jumped on to the floor with a feline grunt. She let out a few pathetic coughs, followed by a loud retch, and deposited a half digested mackerel onto the wooden floor.

"I just thought you should know," said Sheryl, and without even waiting for my reply or finishing her coffee, left.

I stared down at Puss, my guilt and shame complete; Puss cleaned her ears and then made for her cat flap and I was alone, with the horrible thought that there was only me to pick up the mackerel.

Chapter Six

THE READ AND BE THANKFUL

A Zimmer frame is only as good as the person who uses it.

Rodger and I took it in turns to run the shop, and two days after my verbal assault on Mavis it was my turn. I had to brave Lochgilphead and serve in the Read and be Thankful.

When Rodger first bought the shop, he had this idea of creating Lochgilphead's answer to Waterstones in a rustic style. The shop is single-fronted and not that large, but somehow he managed to fit a corduroy couch and a Nescafé machine into it. Everything was beige and brown, with the odd yellow splashed about. Not my choice, but this is the west of Scotland where square sausages are the norm, and brown sauce is considered a condiment; brown is everywhere.

I left the cottage and walked along the Crinan Canal. I had a lot to think about, mainly how and when should I face Mavis again and when I did, what would I say? Frosty mornings are good for that- trying not to slip on ice can be very focusing.

The footpath was empty except for a dog walker skidding behind his energetic trio of collies and a crazy jogger with the sort of stoical face that gives being healthy a bad name. I crossed the front street and headed along to the Co-op car park, and skidded, full-blown, both legs like any four legged creature you can think of on ice. I lurched from one car to another with a loud scream and looked up to see the jogger continue by with a smirk. It wasn't easy regaining dignity after that, even a friendly wave and a "you alright?" from the postie didn't help, especially when he had the cheek to carry on.

I looked down at my bag with all its contents splayed out on the ice and started to pick them up when a grimy hand began to help.

"Don't rush," she said, "get your breath back."

I knew before I saw her that it was the Bag Lady, a homeless woman who had taken to sitting outside the Co-op entrance on a shabby tartan blanket . She had arrived in Lochgilphead the day Rodger was celebrating his revamped Read and be Thankful with an open day. Rodger's passion for sheds had obviously been burning deep inside him for a long time, and about a year ago he decided to renovate the shop with a more manly 'I love sheds' look.

I had no idea where that would eventually lead.

The day of the grand opening, I went into the Stables to give them an earful about their so-called finger buffet, and there was the Bag Lady or 'co-op Bag Lady', as she sometimes known as sitting outside the Stables on the concrete with her black hair pulled into a bun, tight enough to stretch her leathery face into a makeshift face lift. She had a back pack on her back and was tucking into a roll and sausage a passer-by had given her. *I remember it because her shoes were tatty enough to make me throw a two pound coin instead of fifty pence onto her blanket.*

"The more you have the less you hold," she shouted.

I struggled to get myself together, not easy when you have the Co-op Bag Lady's face looking down at you. And I was about to offer a *thanks but I can manage* comment when she said "Mind how you go, there are cars everywhere." I looked up at the old woman, *what would she know?* I stood up and made for the street.

"Hey," she shouted again. "Mind the bus."

Cars, now buses; in Lochgilphead where the traffic was as frequent as the part-time parking attendant? I left her one of my, 'I've crossed roads all my life and I'm still standing' looks and was just about to step out onto the road, when a bus the size of a freight train passed by driving way past the speed limit. I froze. I was nearly part of the tarmac.

I was about to mumble "cheers" when she shouted, "Mind the van."

I spent the day serving romantic novels and cook books and when quiet, dipping into my *Dare to be Nice* book, all the time hoping that Mavis would come in to help and then hoping she wouldn't. I was in a constant state of flux punctuated by the Bag Lady's singing, in fact I was just in the middle of pondering the possible intelligence of the Bag Lady when Mavis walked in and dumped my unreturned Amazon parcels on the shop desk.

She said nothing, but took one look at me sweating over an abnormally long till receipt and sighed. She wanted attention. I could feel it, hear it in her chubby fingers now drumming on the counter.

I decided to look her straight in the eye, and she looked back without a word, Mavis always has a word to say. I was worried, what was her game? Was she here to give me a mouthful? Gloat? Tell me again how marvellous Zumba was or call me an alcoholic? I watched her pick up a Jamie Oliver and pretend to browse.

"How was your last class?" she said without a glance in my direction.

"Adequately attended," I muttered.

"I heard different."

I could tell by the way she flicked that she had something planned. But I didn't want to stoop to asking. Mavis could spend all day flicking if she wanted, I wasn't going to break. I waited and waited, until finally...I heard herself, the Bag Lady singing *Come on Eileen* again. How a woman parked outside the Co-op playing on a small battery operated keyboard could be heard through the town was beyond me. But her shrill voice was louder than a car alarm, and it filled the silence between me and Mavis like an organ at a funeral, I wanted to kiss her or at least shake her hand...

I flashed my best smile at Mavis. "Do you remember when the Stable's asked her to leave?"

"No."

"She moved to the Baptist church and sung there for a while. Remember when we went to the coffee morning and she wanted to read your palm?"

Mavis sighed, "she was there for a day until someone tried to convert her."

"And the golf course, do you remember when she sang songs for the Vietnam veterans " I faked a laugh.

"Someone lobbed a ball at her," said Mavis, "I wouldn't call that funny in fact I think she had a few stitches."

"Oh."

"But at least they apologized."

"Yes."

"Pick a winner and you're a loser" shouted the Bag Lady.

"Sheryl reckons I should apologise," I finally muttered.

Mavis stopped at a stuffing recipe and pretended to read, allowing my comments to remain in the air like stale wind.

"I had a few the other night," I said "I know... but...and....I ...think I was a little out of order..."

Mavis snapped the book shut, "According to Lumpy, you're going through a rough patch."

"Lumpy?" I said.

"Yes," our eyes met, she didn't break.

"The other night I was trying to centre myself," I muttered "not a great thing to do in a pub."

"Perhaps you should give up the pub for a while, try a detox. We are on a sugar-free month," she said.

"What?"

"Lumpy's idea."

"Who?"

"We are clearing out all things sugary from the cupboards."

Lumpy and her were giving up sugar, together? I didn't know what to say.

"Yes, cut sugar out and you're laughing that's what Lumpy says".

Mavis was using her patronising tone, the one she used in the post office for dithering pensioners struggling with the card machine and it was beginning to grate.

"Look if you've come here to chew my ear off, just say it, get it over with?"

She didn't answer; instead she started to tell me about Shifty hooking up with some fabulous artist, like I was interested. Then, with absolutely no expression whatsoever, she pulled out a poster from her bag, and slid it onto the counter.

Zumba is Exotic
Zumba is Fun
Zumba is Here
at
Ardrishaig Gala Day

I looked at the poster. The illustrations were familiar – too familiar. It was decorated in an art nouveau style typical of Rodger. My Rodger, who hadn't painted in years, was now, it seemed, drawing for a woman who he claimed had as much personality as a Twix bar. I wondered what would happen if I asked him why. Would he tell me or just walk into the shed with the same swing of his hips that Mavis had now seemed to adopt?

I looked at Mavis questioningly.

"Rodger's cool with it," she finally said.

Cool; Mavis saying cool is as plausible as the Pope shouting, 'let's hear it for Durex!' Who was she trying to impress? I stared at the stinking poster in front of me which was probably in every shop from here to Tarbert. She honestly thought that I would put it up in the shop where I spend most of my days.

I picked up the poster and scrunched it into a ball. "This," I said, holding the ball of art nouveau bullshit in the air, "is going where Rodger's shed plans ended up."

Mavis watched me shove the now screwed up poster into the bin. "There's no need for that," she said. "I was only trying to help."

"Help with what? Destroying my classes, rubbing my nose in it?"

I watched my ex-student take the screwed up poster and flatten it out. "I just thought you'd like to try a class, you'd pick it up no problem. Imogen is an amazing teacher. She could teach your Puss to dance if she wanted to. And besides, it might help with your drinking. That's what Lumpy says..."

I pulled the poster from her and shoved it back in the bin. "Bugger Lumpy and bugger you, and as for picking it up, I would rather pick up a parking ticket than your Zumba and I don't drink that much..."

Mavis tutted, "Lumpy said it was too soon."

"Too soon for what?"

"For being nice, he said you'd shove it back in my face," she said.

I stared at her and she stared back, our eyes locked, neither giving in – even when a customer clattered in with her Zimmer frame, saw the two of us, muttered an 'oh' and then clattered out again. Even when the phone rang we continued to stare, like cats in an alleyway.

"You never did like my dancing, did you?" she said.

"It's not a case of liking," I muttered.

"Imogen has me in the front row. She says I am a natural."

"Natural? Anyone can be natural doing jumping jacks to a thumping beat."

"She says my hips are on fire," said Mavis, and grabbed the poster from me. "And Lumpy has even videoed me."

"Bed socks are only as good as the feet inside them." Shouted the Co-op bag lady.

I grabbed it back, and it ripped. Mavis tossed what was left in her hands onto the counter and turned to leave. She walked to the door and opened it, *Come on Eileen* echo through the streets....

"You know, not all of us are goddesses like you, but you could have just once, *just once*, given me something more to do than stand at the back waving a scarf around."

She looked so defiant, and strong,

"But you wave the scarf like a real pro...you with a scarf was the best," I said, *and I meant it*.

"Typical, just typical, and you think you're being nice," she said, "Well you can shove it."

I stared at my pal we had had fall outs before, but she had never told me to shove anything...I watched her walk into the street leaving the door swinging and a faint whiff of Tweed behind. I waited for her to look back. I walked to the window and watched, but she didn't, instead she jumped into Imogen's car and stared in front of her as they drove off.

Chapter Seven

CHUBBY, A WOMANLY BUTCHER

Beware of what you write; it may come back miss-spelled.

That night, as I sat alone on our white couch, I thought about the hair of the dog or chocolate, but the shop was closed, and Rodger's homebrew was hidden, locked and accounted for, probably somewhere in the shed. So instead, to revel in misery I flicked over the *Fyne News* like a gull flicking over debris with only a herbal to console me. I was halfway through choking down a cranberry tea when in walked Kay and Sheryl with a few of Steven's homemade chocolate slices. They had decided to cheer me up. The *Fyne News* had a full two-page spread dedicated to a look back at some of those fantastic Zumba days, as well as their Gala day debut, and according to Kay, they knew I would be torturing myself with it.

Chubby had surpassed herself this time, with an overdramatic article titled...*The Storming Of Zumba*. Which Kay read out in her usual sarcastic tone; "*written by, Chubby, Lochgilphead's long-standing and favourite butcher.*" I am sure she made the last bit up.

"Zumba has stormed into Lochgilphead like a freight train and has swept the females up like an eagle with a lamb. Imogen bounces where others would never dare," read out Kay, "Zumba has put the pulse back into the community centre with its sizzling moves to Latin American beats. It is a dance for all."

It was a painful article to read with over the top comments from many students including ex Weight Watcher Betty finally losing weight with '*Imogen's inspirational teachings.*' And how Mavis '*our very own post office lady*' had '*finally found a dance for all,*' with '*No props, no scarves, just you, your teacher and a whole load of new friends,*' *a* comment that I must have read at least three times before Kay and Sheryl had arrived.

"If only you'd let her do more than wave a scarf," muttered Sheryl.

On the same page as the article were photos of Imogen wearing a bright pink 'Zumba rocks' t-shirt surrounded by school children, at her free *Zumba for children* day; Imogen sitting by a chirpy looking elderly man while wearing a purple 'real men Zumba' t-shirt at her *you're never too old to Zumba* day; and Imogen, along with a few others, standing by the checkout in the Co-op. They, along with the shop assistant, were wearing a pink 'Zumba never forgets' t-shirt. They were bag packing for charity, for poor people in some South American country where it all started. To quote the great stick insect, 'They gave us Zumba, it's time we gave something back!'

It was, I have to say, one of Chubby's most over the top pieces she had ever written, which she followed up with an interview with the *wonderful human being*, stating that "*Zumba challenges the body, the mind and the spirit,*" and "*how we all could benefit from a little mindful salsa.*"

Kay closed the paper with a "what a load of tosh" comment. "I don't think you have anything to worry about," she continued. "I mean, look how quickly belly dancing came and went."

"What?"

"Well, everything is a fad when it comes to dance and fitness. I mean, how many of us have one of those exercise balls rolling about the spare room?"

"Dance and fitness? Belly dance is more than that, it's a way of life."

"So is Zumba, according to Chubby's article."

"Zumba has taken everything... including my Rodger!" I pulled out the two bits of the poster. "He's painting again."

"And?" said Kay.

"With her!"

No one said anything.

"He's gone to the other side."

Kay threw Sheryl a look.

When I first met Rodger, he liked to watch me dance, and I felt like I was sixteen again. No one had looked at me for years and there he was not only loving me, but asking me to dance. Back then in the good old days we spent evenings together listening to dance music; Cheb Mami was one of his favourites. Rodger would unplug the phone, light a few candles, tell me what to wear or what not to, and then sit back on our white couch and watch me dance. He was so inspired that he began to paint me rather than his usual landscapes. He became a man possessed, and soon a whole collection of work was produced. Within months I was in colour, on canvases larger than a front door, in pastels, oils, and he wanted to put them in a show. He even had me, his *Flower of Scotland*, tattooed on his left shoulder.

"When a man paints you over and over again and then makes an exhibition of those paintings it is hard not to miss the attention." I said.

"It's just a poster," said Kay.

"I mean it wasn't my fault they didn't sell, that no one wanted a picture of me belly dancing. I thought Rodger's *Flower of Scotland* exhibition was amazing, once you got used to them."

"Don't you think it's a good thing he is painting again?" said Sheryl.

"Yes but it's not me; is it?" I said.

Kay and Sheryl looked unimpressed...it's not the first time they had told me I was "self-obsessed".

"And I blame that bloody shed," I said. "That shed has transformed him into a stranger, especially whenever I venture near or even mention the shed. Once I knocked on the door and told him his nut roast was ready and waiting and he told me to stuff it, claiming he was otherwise engaged and a nut roast was the least of his worries. Then he turned up the music over some sort of chanting. Who chants in a shed, on their own, and on an empty stomach?"

Sheryl tried to stop me with a 'we all change' comment.

"And then there was the day I merely suggested that I could store some of my dancing equipment in the shed, and he went ballistic with a 'can I not have any bollocking space to call my own,' answer. He shouted so loud his veins were sticking out of his neck! My Rodger has always been a placid man. Call centres never bothered him, drivers who never indicated didn't bother him... God knows how he would react now. And then, one evening, my Rodger came into the kitchen with a stupid explanation that he would from now on be sleeping in the shed, for artistic reasons. 'I can't breathe and you are suffocating me, you and your goddess bullshit!' he said and flounced out. Bullshit, I ask you! Even Puss felt for me, I could tell."

"She's just a cat," said Kay.

"I'm so confused. I've lost my soul mate. To be with a man who no longer wants to share my bed is rubbish... more than rubbish, it has put me off my pelvic tilts."

I stared out into the patio at the clipped lawn. At least he still mowed the grass. "I said to him 'what's wrong with the couch?' and he burst into some tirade about my drinking and inability to sing properly."

Kay called me melodramatic; no surprises there, she is tough. She is the sort of woman who is comfortable in a garage, beating down the price of an oil change. Melodramatic to her is anything along the lines of a repeated moan. "I showed him the poster," I finally said.

"And what did he say?"

"He picked it up and said 'not one of my best works but it paid for the veranda for the shed.' I couldn't believe he was so flippant. 'Doesn't our Flower of Scotland mean anything to you?' I asked."

"And what did he say?"

"Nothing. Shifty had arrived with solar power lights for the veranda."

"Oh."

"Much more important."

"And now he, along with the tattoo of yours truly, is sleeping in a rustic colour dog kennel of a shed, with solar powered lights. He's like a ghost, a faint noise at the other end of the garden who leaves notes telling me to work in the shop." I started crying. "That shop, and its fucking shed posters."

Sheryl got up and boiled the kettle, while Kay pushed a packet of tissues my way.

"I feel lost," I muttered.

Kay pulled out a tissue and wiped her eyes. "Chocolate, anyone?"

Chapter Eight

THE CO-OP BAG LADY AND THE THIEF

To catch a thief is as easy as catching a mouse...

A few days later Sheryl and Kay took me to the Stables. We were being served by Bessie. Bessie had been to many of my classes years ago. She had the sort of curves that had many an elderly gentleman reaching for their beta blockers. She was a real asset back then, and unlike turncoat Mavis, she didn't leave my classes for Zumba. She joined the self-assertiveness class for women and has stood up to the chef, demanding proper fitting uniforms, and name badges. So far they had one, *'Bessie is your waitress'* badge to share and extra-large shirts were on order.

Bessie plonked my machine-made latte in front of me and as I wiped the dribble from the side of the glass she started to moan about the Bag Lady. The Co-op Bag Lady was singing extra loud that day, so loud that her voice could be heard over Radio One playing in the kitchen, despite it being turned up twice, and the chef was talking of phoning the police.

"What do you expect from a woman like her...she's from travelling stock, she probably had to yell all her life," said Kay.

"Either that or she's deaf," I said.

Everyone talked about the Bag Lady, rumors ran like water down a drain. Some say she comes from old money, others that she slept in the graveyard and others that she could predict the future purely by watching the morning traffic.

"Of course herself in the kitchen," said Bessie, "reckons she used to sell her body", *(a comment which no one took seriously, even the couple opposite who up to this time were engrossed in their fish supper.)* "But then herself in there, thinks *Coronation Street* is a documentary."

"That'll be right", yelled the chef bursting from the kitchen like an army cook. Her round face looked red and angry and her apron looked like she had been cooking in a temper for a week. "What's the social doing?" she said. "All those empty houses up the brae. Why don't they just shove her in there? I mean, I'm sick to death of trying to shop and stepping over her stuff. Of course, some folk have started shopping at Tesco. Not me, she'll not stop me."

The chef then retreated, barking at Bessie to 'get herself in here!' which had as much effect on Bessie as my dancing did on Rodger, Bessie pulled up a chair and asked us how we knew *herself- The Bag lady*.

Kay talked about the golf course incident, and how she, despite being a pacifist, and *"if old enough would have been up there burning her bra with Jane Fonda "* did her best to stop the lobbing of golf balls.

"No one deserves to die by a capitalist instrument of leisure", said Kay confusing both Bessie and the fish supper couple.

Sheryl talked about how the Co-op Bag Lady loitered outside the library several afternoons until her mother, Beatrice who works in the library tried to run her over with her wheelchair.

"She was one of the few people to get the better of my mother," said Sheryl.

Even Kay was impressed, after all telling someone in a wheel chair that they don't know how to drive it, in the disabled parking area, in front of a district nurse is, as the radio one loving chef would say was *"asking for it!"*

My first real run in with the Bag Lady was months ago - pre-shed days, back in the days when Rodger and I spent time together. I was preparing for my dwindling belly dance class. I was on the couch in *The Read and be Thankful* with my laptop, working on some choreography for the Gala Day – *if only I knew* – and Rodger was heading for the bank with the week's takings. He had just finished a latte made by my own hands and was packing things up. Neither of us took much notice of the baby-faced blond boy with Itsie a tiny ball of a terrier with little hair. It seems that the innocent looking blond had planned it for weeks. Young Blondie had been in the shop before and had apparently *cased* the joint, although what there was to case is hard to know; just Rodger and a bag of money heading for the bank, and my laptop.

Young Blondie had been in and out of the shop all morning, lurking about the self-help section, which at the time I thought was a funny thing for a young man to be interested in. But as soon as Rodger was heading out the door, he changed and moved towards the romance section, picking up a novel with a lurid cover. It had me wondering – even I wouldn't want to read that.

I was just about to ask if he wanted help when he shouted 'what the fuck!' while pointing behind my head. I looked and he grabbed my laptop with all my dances on it.

I yelled- a lot.

Rodger turned around as Blondie made for the door. I grabbed Blondie's shoulder and pulled him back; he collapsed on top of me and we both fell onto the couch. He wrenched himself from me and stumbled into the desk, disrupting several paperbacks.

Rodger raced back into the shop, forgetting about his money bag. And that's when, like a worm, Itsy, edged his way from under the self-help section and took the takings from Rodger's hand. Blondie picked up the bowl of complimentary toffees and scattered them onto the floor and then pushed the *Travel Scotland* postcard stand over, covering the entrance in a sea of tartan Scottish maps. Mavis who had just arrived froze in the doorway. She started shouting 'mind the toffees; mind the dog; oh heavens; get the dog,' until Blondie pushed her into the travel section and bolted.

Rodger skidded on the *Travel Scotland* tartan and nearly stood on Mavis who was now prostrate between the travel section and the front door, and he too bolted.

"What's going on?" said Mavis adjusting herself, but I had no time to answer; I wanted my dances back and from the smell of cigarette coming from Blondie, I reckoned I had a good chance of catching up with him. Five minutes up that road and he'd be coughing like an eighty–year-old asthmatic. I pushed Mavis back into the travel section and followed.

By this time, the shop alarm was ringing and, as with a car alarm, no one batted an eye. Not even the few children loitering about the shop, the same children who had tormented the Bag Lady on the miniature golf green. And when they saw Blondie running by they began to shout. Rodger followed the boy, and I followed both as they passed the shop and the Bag Lady.

I was livid; all my dances... But I was catching up I have the thighs of a belly dancer and I was almost on top of Blondie when the Bag Lady stuck her leg out as Blondie ran by and I pushed- like a sack of potatoes; he went down with Rodger on top, while Itsie disappeared round the corner.

There was an undignified scuffle after they both landed on the blanket, sending some coins rolling into all directions.

'Fight! Fight! Fight!' yelled some of the kids, while others made for the coins as the two men rolled about like a couple of four-year-olds in mud, except they were on her grubby blanket, and it was flapping about unsettling what looked like a decade of dust. Rodger started to cough, and Blondie tried to take advantage. I pushed him down on the concrete and held him there.

Like I said,I have the thighs of a belly dancer − we have muscles where you wouldn't believe. And as I sat astride him, I used every taut and overworked leg muscle I had to immobilise him. He could hardly breathe. And he looked scared; no self-help book would have prepared him for that situation.

I was about to shout one of our dance war cries *for added drama* when the Co-op door opened. The assistant manager came out with several packets of Andrex under his arm and saw a middle-aged woman astride a frightened looking young man. He had the look of someone who had just caught his granny watching *Fifty Shades of Grey*.

"What's going on?" he yelled.

He looked at the herd of children standing around cheering like a mob at a fight club, and tried to gain some sort of control. Not easy when you're no larger than the children you're shouting at, with a shop uniform swimming on your frame like an un-pegged tent.

"Clear off!" he shouted.

The children started laughing. "I said, get out of it!" he continued and chucked a toilet roll at them, no one moved.

He stared at us through his Clark Kent glasses. By this time, Rodger was up and looking about for the dog, realising that his takings for the week were gone. I had Blondie pinned to the ground with my knee. He looked terrified and was actually asking Rodger for help, but I wasn't letting go.

"Get your own bloody laptop," I shouted.

The manager pulled me off the boy. "Have you no shame?"

"It's mine," I shouted, as Rodger continued to mutter along the lines of 'where the hell is that bloody dog?'

And then from around the corner, like a firefighter holding a pup in a Diet Coke advert, walked Shifty with the thieving terrier. He looked particularly handsome in a bit of rough sort of way. He was wearing a slim fitting green shirt that seemed to have lost half its buttons and a pair of way too tight jeans. Apparently he was in the middle of redecorating the reception and fancied one of Chubby's vegetarian sausages. He ran around the corner and, as the wind ruffled his blond hair, it blew open his shirt just enough to make Mavis, who had appeared from nowhere, mutter, "Oh my."

He looked, rough, arrogant and interesting, Lochgilphead's answer to Mr Darcy and Rodger's face lit up.

I shouted something about the takings over Blondie's heaving chest. But Rodger didn't answer, he didn't even look at me; he just stared at Shifty like he had never seen him before, despite the fact that we had been in the Argyll many times.

Itsie was wearing a guide dog jacket. Apparently, that's what gave him away. As he ran past Chubby's butcher shop, Shifty was standing in the doorway; hearing the shop alarm and seeing a dog with a way too large guide dog jacket swinging about his waist made Shifty think.

"Chubby, quick, some mince," he shouted. Chubby threw the closest thing to hand and the dog was putty in Shifty's hands.

From that moment on all I heard from Rodger was 'Shifty this' and 'Shifty that' and 'what a great guy Shifty was' and 'how Shifty does this and not that'. The next thing I knew, Rodger was picking up a flat pack shed at the post office and Shifty was not only giving him a lift but helping him unwrap it like a Christmas present.

"They are very thick, your Rodger and Shifty, aren't they?" said Bessie.

I looked at her; I had never really thought about it and to be honest I didn't want to think about it. And when Bessie started to talking about the Shifty self-assertiveness classes and how Rodger was his favourite student, the macaroni in my stomach began to churn.

I watched Bessie finally disappear into the kitchen and the door swing behind her.

"Chubby's bit of silverside has a lot to answer for," said Kay, causing the couple opposite to chuckle over their tartare sauce, and the macaroni in my stomach to churn again.

Chapter Nine

MAVIS AND LUMPY

Showing off is not only for show offs.

The girls, it seems, were now hell bent on organising my life into some sort of positive rebirth. Sheryl and Kay's treat at the Stables had been a ruse to butter me up, seduce me into accepting the offer of judging for the WRI at the Gala day, Kay's idea of me facing up to things.

"After all" as Kay put it, "If the Co-op Bag lady can stand up to Sheryl's Beatrice and the district nurse, you can look Zumba in the eye and carry on living."

Apparently Iona, who organised most groups in the area for women, loved my free workshop from a while back and thought I would do a 'smashing job' of handing out the prizes for the coat hanger section, as long as I 'gave the goddess thing a miss'.

And Kay, it seems, had the idea of *gently breaking me in* by meeting the day before.

I wasn't in the mood, watching Lumpy and Mavis setting up the Banner for Zumba with the army-like precision of a couple who spent a lot of time together, was the last thing I felt like doing...

"I'd rather have root canal treatment done by the roads department," I said.

Sheryl told me not to be so dramatic.

"And we were never allowed a banner" I added, "Which everyone seems to forget."

Kay reminded me as a teacher to a child that I didn't want one, "you said we- sorry -you were enough."

I caved in after that...

We watched Mavis and Lumpy unroll the banner onto the ground. She was posing in her new purple over grey look, her new image from my old clothes, *Rodger said he was 'sick of purple and would rather see me in a potato sack than another purple outfit.'* Everything matched, from her purple on blond streaks ruffling in the wind to her purple clip-ons, large and Mexican looking, probably the Zumba taking hold.

"Purple is the colour of passion," she loved to say.

At the time I thought it was for some imaginary Egyptian man in some future trip to Egypt, now it seems it was for Lumpy. And Lumpy appeared to enjoy the look. With a hammer in his hand and nails between his lips, he was up and down the ladder with a jaunty bounce that I had never seen before. Occasionally he shouted, 'Is this alright?' or 'What do you think?' Nobody cared, apart from Mavis or Mav, as he was now calling her. And Mav was enthralled, like he was creating some sort of masterpiece and she was handing him tools of great importance.

Lumpy had changed right before my eyes and I hadn't even noticed. Six months ago, if you had said Lumpy was boyfriend material I would have laughed into my cappuccino. No one would look at Lumpy as partner material. He was the sort that everybody knew, and no one would want to date, who had no life apart from loitering at the community centre filling up the tea urn and shouting at kids for wasting toilet paper- an event was not an event without him present. But now, since he and Mavis hit it off Lumpy is a new man with a new life, no more roll-ups or coughing, no more shouting at kids- Mavis had brought back the Elvis in him.

Kay introduced me to Iona who stood in the car park watching everything like she had organised it all. She was taller and slimmer than

I remember with the same 'grey hair and I am proud of it' cut and loose jeans that still made me jealous.

"I have been hip circling ever since, works wonders on the thighs for riding,' she laughed, followed by reminiscing about my ability to teach with a pencil which, although many laughed at, was not 'her cup of tea.'

"Teaching women how to circle their hips isn't easy." I said, "And if telling them to imagine a pencil between their thighs drawing a circle on the ground helps, then so be it."

Iona patted me on the cheek with "absolutely" and moved on to the fire department that was setting up their stall next to her *live baking* tent.

"Wouldn't your flammable show be better over there by the Zumba banner," she smiled. "It will be like you're on stage- everyone could see you."

Lumpy had heard all about the pencil. He had been in our class more than once to 'bleed the radiators'. Once he 'bled a radiator' right through a whole class. At the time, I was guiding the girls through drawing with your pencil: a circle, a square, a W and finally their name. Women were shifting and sliding their pelvises to the music, lost in the movement and oblivious to Lumpy's presence.

The Lumpy of old had always been invisibly present...

Lumpy stopped coming into my class once Mavis left, and, probably by the look of Mav's rapt attention, had his own pencil show now.

"Imogen doesn't need any pencil," said Mavis, with her back to us. "Or any other cheap tricks."

"That's because Zumba isn't as complex," shouted Kay.

"Zumba can be complex, can't it, Lumpy?" said Mav.

"Well, there's complex and there's complex, Mav, and there is nothing as complex as a woman." Lumpy looked lovingly at Mavis, "and Mav; I am more than happy to explore such complexities."

Mavis handed him more nails with the sort of smile that makes a single woman jealous.

※

That night I went home, pulled out some cold chicken from the fridge and started shredding it for Puss. Mavis and I had done so many things together and now I had lost her to Zumba and Lochgilphead's answer to Elvis. I put on a CD I bought from the last workshop Mavis and I had organised. It was a couple of years ago, in honour of Sheryl and Steven's secret wedding. Lumpy was there organizing the food with Mavis by his side grating carrot to Neil Diamond's *Blue Jeans* ...I hadn't a clue...

Hattie from Greenock was the teacher. She was an athletic woman with a muscular stomach and a drum solo that impressed even the men who were only there under protest to keep their other halves happy. And she was strong. When Lumpy's tea urn fell off its perch during the cool down, she picked it up with one hand and didn't grunt once.

Hattie spent the day teaching a dance no one could follow with the double veil, which no one really got the hang of.

Her workshop was called *Tapping the Power Within*, and her voice was anything but soothing; it was more commanding. She had no time for my pencil theory, in fact I was sent to the back of the class with a 'there is only room for one teacher in this class' comment. She talked about feeling your feet planted firmly on the earth and connecting to the muscles deep within the stomach. And then she took us outside to dance on the sand.

"Close your eyes," she said, "and picture a night in the desert sands around a campfire with just a drum."

Jimmy, a Lebanese drummer, began to play. "Belly dance is the dance of the desert," he said. "It comes from drums and shadows in the night. You have to tell the story with your hips and your arms because your feet can't move in the sand." Jimmy spent years studying the Egyptian drum in Lebanon. And he talked about women who walked the marketplace with only their eyes on show, women who could seduce any man with just a look or a move of a shoulder.

That night at the Hafla, Hattie was now Hatshepsut; unrecognisable, exotic and made up like an Egyptian Queen who, with her eyes and a flick of her shoulder seduced the audience. She performed the dance from her workshop, the dance none of us could remember, let alone do. She controlled her audience; her aggressive hip flicks and stomach pops demanded respect, admiration and quite a few gasps from the men in the audience, and she was older than me.

I slipped on the music of Hatshepsut, *Taht El Shibak* and began to move my hips. "I could do that"… I shouted at Puss.

Puss, unmoved, sniffed at the chicken, pawed it, and then with a look of disdain, sauntered to the cat flap. I thought about the shed. I could improvise; I could re-enact that night and maybe remind Rodger of happier times. I began to circle my hips to the music and bounce the heels of my feet to the beat. If Mavis could pull and reform Lumpy into the man he now is, then imagine what I could do.

And I was sure there was some sand kicking about somewhere.

Chapter Ten

THE GALA DAY

When in doubt, hug a tree.

It was the Gala day and the last place I wanted to be. However, knitted coat hangers were waiting and I was committed, along with Sheryl's Stephen, who had also been asked to hand out prizes for the short story competition, a first for Ardrishaig. It was Chubby's idea. It was her first year on the committee and she was keen to make her mark. The first prize was a story called *I Know a Place Within a Place*, and was set in Lochgilphead, about a female shinty player who wanted to come out. By all accounts it was a touching story and well worth the first prize of being published in the paper, along with a free meat pack from Chubby.

The Gala day was busy; the sun was out, and people were everywhere eating burgers and drinking outside the pub.

The car park near the public toilets was where all the action took place. It was the prime spot because the WRI stand was there, full of every decent type of home baking you could imagine, and they sold the best hot filled rolls for miles.

The ambulance men stood close by, offering free rides for anyone under the age of ten, siren optional, and beside them was an ancient ex-fireman giving an impressive demonstration with fat and water, although it was the same as last year.

As Kay liked to say, "There are only so many ways you can shake a hose."

The church hall was packed with stalls and a Victorian afternoon tea room, which was selling the same WRI baking as on the stall but cut into delicate bite-size pieces and served on cake stands with lace doilies and napkins in rings. There was also a bouncy castle, an old car parade and a miniature train, which took children from the old car parade to the bouncy castle and back again.

The pipe band opened the day with a march down the street behind the Gala queen. By the time I had arrived they had finished playing, and were standing around discussing which pub to go to while shooing away children who were trying to investigate what was really under a kilt.

Everyone looked happy, apart from me.

Steven administered his prize after the bagpipes and Gala queen procession had finished. He stood beside the ambulance men and the firemen and made a small speech about how there is a good story in all of us. I wasn't asked to do a speech, but rather to hop along to the sale of works stall, stick some prize stickers on each coat hanger and try not to leave anyone out.

It took me five minutes to scan the five coat hangers, all of which were so over-decorated that you were lucky to find room to hang a piece of string on. We got a free cup of coffee along with a free egg roll, and a 'nice work, thank you, but I preferred the sock holder' from Iona, who was wearing even looser jeans than the other day.

After the prize-giving, my plan was for a quick exit before Zumba, but the masochist got the better of me; that and the offer of a quick one in the beer tent with Steven and Sheryl. I was just on my second and making plans to leave when I saw the Bag Lady lurking at the back of the church, pushing a supermarket trolley full of bread. She was heading for the Zumba poster. She saw me, looked away, walked on a bit, stopped her trolley, looked back and then with a quick conversation to herself pushed the trolley behind the poster.

"Get ready to rumble. Zumba is here!" shouted the commentator into his handheld mic.

I wanted to go; leave and not torture myself. Failure is hard, rejection painful, and staring at the opposition cheerfully lining up to applause was just reliving all that pain again. Why was I doing it to myself? Clutching a half-eaten egg roll and the remains of a lukewarm beer, I watched Mavis giggling like a schoolgirl with my feet rooted to the spot.

Maybe she'll fall over...

The Zumba girls lined up; there was at least twenty-five of them, three rows of women from as far as Tarbert and Inveraray. Mavis was in the front centre behind Imogen and hardly visible. Imogen's long legs were covered in pink Lycra, and she wore a tight cropped top to show off her flat stomach, while the others behind her were in purple – now my least favourite colour – with baggier t-shirts and no flat stomachs on show.

According to Sheryl, who got it from Mavis over an impressive banoffee pie, Imogen insisted on baggy t-shirts for everyone due to the different sizes in the troupe. Imogen called it kindness; Kay called it Imogen's massive ego; and Mavis was put out. Mavis had spent the last six months doing sit-ups and avoiding bread for just such a moment, to celebrate her firmer stomach.

"Do you want peace of mind?" yelled Imogen.

"YES!!!" from the girls.

"Positive thoughts?" yelled Imogen.

"YES!" from the girls and a few in the audience.

"Your aura and chakras balanced?" said Imogen.

No one answered.

"Let's get Zumba-ing," Imogen shouted, like a born-again evangelist, and the music began to play. 'Zumba, Zumba, Zumba!!'

From behind the ambulance the Bag Lady appeared again, this time with a small goose in her arms. She stared for a minute, and then broke into a jig, still clutching the goose, until another much larger goose appeared and began to peck at her tartan skirt. She pulled a slice of bread from her pocket, waved it in front of the goose's beak and then tossed it behind the poster for the goose to demolish.

Then she disappeared.

The old church sat as a backdrop to the performing Zumba girls; it also overlooked Loch Fyne and the shore. Swinging from the roof of the church was the giant pink and purple Zumba poster that Lumpy and Mav had spent all afternoon hanging; it was large enough to cover the whole side of the church.

The poster was completely over the top, with larger than life images of Imogen and a few of her students, including Mavis, in various stages of jumping jacks. They looked ecstatic, with joyful 'Yippee' sorts of expressions. And splashed at the bottom, under the 'Yippee' jumping jacks, were the words, 'Be all you can be the Zumba way!'

We belly dancers never needed a poster...

Then a swan sauntered out from behind the poster, followed by the Bag Lady flapping her skirt and shooing it away. I heard a few chuckles from behind me.

'Zumba, Zumba, Zumba!!'

The girls started to perform in unison like a purple and pink army.

"Pump it up, ladies, let's go for the burn!" Imogen had a headset on and was shouting like Jane Fonda.

I watched the pink army hoping, wishing, that they weren't so coordinated and professional; wishing one of them would trip, miss a move or at least drop a step, but no, they were almost perfect, even Mavis.

I was just thinking about a third pint or something even stronger or even... leaving! I mean, there was no need for me to see how perfect they were. I am sure I would hear all about it from someone. Then I heard from the back mutterings and sniggers along with, "Will you look at that," type comments.

Four large white swans and a couple of geese emerged from behind the posters, waddling in line. The birds circled about the dancers, and then the swans began to spread their wings while pushing their beaks forward, hissing as the geese squawked.

"Alright, girls, remain calm," said Imogen. No one listened, not even the audience, but Imogen carried on.

And then a goose went right up to Imogen and started to nip at her Lycra. She lashed at it with a 'bugger off' blaring through her microphone.

"I told them not to feed the swans," said someone.

"You can't play around with a swan, they can break an arm," said another.

The birds continued to hiss.

Someone shouted "turn the music off," someone else shouted, "get some bread," and Mavis yelled for Lumpy.

Imogen began to flap the corner of the poster at the geese, which had no effect at all except to make her swear more. Soon Imogen had worked her way through every swear word you could imagine and her head mic caught it all.

It was a sad end for the Zumba and Gala day. By the time someone had found the Bag Lady's bread trolley and Lumpy had arrived, Imogen's poster flapping had seemed to attract rather than scare the swans, which had now backed her into the sound system corner.

A couple of the pipe members, a few beers to the good, decided that it would be a laugh to scare the birds off with a selection of *Braveheart* war cries.

"*Freedom!*" they yelled, running like mad men. The birds went mental and dispersed into the crowd, allowing a tearful Imogen to throw her mic on the ground like a child and swear in private. No one noticed the side of the poster flop from the church wall and swing into the fireman's demonstration, which was still hot. Before anyone had time to shout, '*Bannockburn*' the poster went up in flames.

The ancient ex-fireman valiantly staggered from the beer tent with his stick waving in the air. He got there just in time to poke at the poster, causing it to collapse about the sound system.

The docking station, which was covered in the burning plastic poster, finally stopped playing and blew up. The ambulance men who were standing at the WRI coffee stand tossed their egg rolls to the wind and raced to the scene, and the birds, noticing the free bread, gave up their hissing and started to tuck in.

I should have felt pleased, rejoiced in my arch enemy's downfall, but I didn't as I watched Imogen drown her tears on the shoulder of the ambulance man. I felt sorry for him. Imogen, who looked pretty good before the fire, was now a mess of black mascara, wet tissues and snot. She had no idea how to cry well, and the ambulance man's shoulder was getting the brunt of it.

"That Bag Lady should be locked up," she blubbered, while blowing like a whale on the ambulance man's tissue. Imogen crying was not a pretty sight.

After I finished my pint, I left. The last thing I felt like doing was helping Sheryl and Steven, along with the Zumba crowd, clear up the mess.

I walked back to the shop and there was the Bag Lady; she was sitting on her blanket with an open packet of bread and a goose egg in her lap. She had made my day and the least I could do was offer her a coffee and some toffees.

Chapter Eleven

THE SHED

All locked up and nowhere to go

In the past belly dancing had given me the strength to leave my old life and my ex. There is nothing more empowering than performing in front of a rugby team's night out or a hen do with people half your age cheering you on, buying you drinks and asking you back. Being wanted after a performance is so empowering, especially when you are using a body too old for procreating.

But even more empowering than that is surviving the gig that failed, leaving a silent room feeling strong, with an 'I did it anyway' exit. Belly dance has always given me results worth dancing for and has always stood me in good stead.

So that night after the Gala day and a few of Rodger's nettle drams, I, inspired by Hattie from Greenock, made a plan of seduction any belly dancer would be proud of. I organised a tight red outfit with a selection of scarves and then like all great performers I slipped on *Immortal Egypt,* music to inspire, and began to visualise myself as the Queen of the Clyde. I fell asleep and dreamed about me seducing like the great Scottish Cleopatra that I wanted to be.

The Cleopatra with mountains of fans cheering, and applauding for me. The vision, the dancing queen; watched all over the world on YouTube. A phenomenon, defying menopause, whose hips outshine those much younger.

I imagine a surge of power within my loins, racing through my thighs, igniting my belly and setting my hips on fire...

And then I see the shed; I open it and walk inside. It is full of candles blowing in the wind and my seduction takes Rodger's breath away.

"Darling, look what you have been missing," I whisper, as my scarves flutter from my body like rose petals.

"God, how I have missed you," he smiles, and comes to me with his arms outstretched.

"I haven't finished," I say. "I have a dance for you." As I push him down on a chair, I begin my dance...

I woke to an annoying purr and belch from Puss. She was sitting on my stomach, and was looking up at me with a 'where is my breakfast?' expression. I stared down at her and she meowed.

When I saw the light on in Rodger's shed, I knew that he was ready, and that was my cue. I put Taht El Shibak on my iPod and sat the station just outside the kitchen door.

Taht El Shibak is a song of a woman looking out of her window lusting after a man. She is seductive and inviting - perfect for me...

I was dressed and ready.

I was really pleased with my costume; my eyes were all that was on show. I had wrapped my eastern pashmina around me like a nomadic dancer of the desert and my face was all but covered by a matching scarf. Underneath was the surprise. I was dressed like an Egyptian Queen in red, gold and blue.

I walked down the path. The intro was a low pulsing rhythm that went on for ages, so I had to take my time; not hard when you have a cat weaving in and out of your feet. Puss couldn't resist the flow of silk; and as she tripped me over yet again I began to curse. Why didn't I save some of that chicken? Chicken is like dope to her, one bowlful gulped down in seconds has her sleeping for days.

I gave her a flick with my foot, and she then took a swipe at my pashmina, getting her claw stuck.

Bollocks! Bugger!

I gave her another kick, but she was determined, and so was I.

Don't look down, look up like a queen. I kept walking slower and slower, waiting for the right moment in the song to do the Hatshepsut move.

When the moment eventually came, I pushed open the shed with my hips and manoeuvred my bottom into position so that it was all that Rodger could see. Then I wiggled seductively, invitingly. What man could resist such an open invitation? By now the music was loud and I pictured Hatshepsut giving me a big thumbs up.

The wiggle turned into a circle and as I edged my way into the shed I did a few more hip moves followed by a Hatshepsut back bend, which, if positioned the right way, gives an amazing view of your cleavage. And as I came up I, inspired by Marilyn Munroe, pursed my lips, *as practised in the mirror*, kicked off my Asda sandals, and I ran my hand up my legs.

Of course I couldn't leave it there; I had to finish the dance. I unwound my scarf while turning a few circles, knocking over this and that, but I knew it didn't matter because I had now woken the animal in Rodger; I could feel his heavy breathing.

I stopped. I could hear other music drowning out my beautiful, seductive belly dancing track.

Dancing Queen?

ABBA was drowning out my music, and Rodger was standing in front of a canvas with his paintbrush upright and poised. He was wearing one of those novelty plastic aprons that men wear when cooking at barbeques.

"What are you doing?" he said.

"I thought I would surprise you," I muttered, trying to remain in temptress pose.

"I see."

"I was doing the dance that you always liked."

The door slammed shut, and Rodger muttered, "Bugger."

I looked at the canvas. "You're painting?" I said.

"Yes."

I fell silent; I could feel my heart thumping. Rodger was painting more stuff, and not just posters? The shed was full of paintings. I didn't know what to say, how had I not known?

"It's very different," I finally muttered.

It was nothing like his previous work. His Flower of Scotland work was mystical, romantic, expressive but very realistic. And before that he painted traditional landscapes, like the old masters, oils on canvas that sat in living rooms. This was an abstract and you really had to look at it for a while to find the subject. When I did, I was dumbstruck.

"Is that a man?" I finally said.

"Yes."

I put my hand on the door; it had slammed shut tight and wouldn't budge.

"It locked," said Rodger, "I had it wedged open but your ...dance buggered that up." Rodger switched the music off and stood with his hands on his hips. "This is the new me," he finally said.

I liked the old Rodger better.

"Bugger the books, bugger the shop. I am a new me," he said, waving his brush in the air.

"What do you mean, the new me? How does someone become a new me?"

Rodger gestured about the shed with an 'isn't it obvious?' look.

"What, just because you're painting again?" I looked about the shed. "Unrecognisable abstracts?"

"You never did get my art, did you?" he muttered.

The shed seemed claustrophobic, oppressive and I just wanted to get out, and out of my stupid queen outfit. And the damn CD was still playing outside and now Puss was on the roof. It seemed as if slamming the door in her face was not taken in the spirit it was meant and she was now parading about on the roof, which had set the dog next door barking.

I tried to open the door again. "Shifty will be here soon," he said.

The dog was a German Shepherd. Once he started barking it would be hours before he'd stop. And within five minutes the noise started working its way right through my head like a drill. I don't know which was worse: the noise of the dog; Rodger standing in his stupid apron like a ponce; or me, standing in an Egyptian Queen outfit with a cleavage no one was interested in.

So we both looked out of the window as Puss began to meow.

Jason, an irritating ten year-old, came out of the house next door. The door slammed hard and then Jason started to imitate his father in a deep voice. "Simmer down, boy," and "that will do," followed by a smack over the head with a rolled up newspaper. My heart bled for the poor dog. Being hit on the head was bad enough, but with the *Daily Record?*

Jason threw a stick at Go Boy, and the dog continued to bark, which was a relief as Rodger and I had nothing to say. We stared anywhere but at each other, as I tried the door again but as Rodger pointed out it was a design fault which up to now had not been a problem.

"Simmer down, boy, or you'll get this on your fucking head," Jason shouted.

Rodger stared out of the pocket-sized window. "Poor dog, trapped like that."

I cried for the rest of that day and the next. I cried for Scotland, England, and pretty much the whole of the English-speaking world after the shed fiasco. I lay on my bed and wept like a film star in the '50s, except there was no background music and no one to comfort me. I couldn't bear to tell anyone.

For the first time in a long time I felt stupid, unwanted and ashamed, and I couldn't face standing in the shop. The only company I had was Puss, who brought a dead mouse into the bedroom, looked at me, took it out again and then curled up on the crumpled Egyptian costume.

I was alone and so I went to bed. Not to sleep, but to hide. The humiliation of the 'new' Rodger and Shifty seeing me in my seduction outfit, of them witnessing my futile plan, was too much to face. I tried mindful breathing, visualisation and even full-on meditation. Nothing worked; my mind was churning. What was I going to do? How could I make things better?

Hot tears came and went, filling up in my eyes until they were puffy; every time I thought about my precious song being taken over by ABBA, I started to cry again. My mind began to race like a hamster on a wheel, fears I hadn't thought about in years raced around in my head. And I could feel the pain of panic, of nothingness, loneliness, of a world without Rodger and his love. I would be nothing and nobody again. Just a middle-aged woman people asked out for coffee out of pity.

Why would he paint abstracts, what was wrong with me? I thought we were together, united with my dream of belly dancing; and that he understood me and my needs.

"My Rodger is not that man anymore," I said. Puss looked up, hopeful, I suspect, of being fed. "That is not my Rodger," I repeated weakly. Puss knew what that meant, more crying and no food. She sighed, jumped up on the bed and slid her head under my hand. My stomach churned into knots as I began to gasp for breath. "All this drama and hardly an audience in sight," I muttered to Puss, who purred under my hand.

In my heart I knew that Rodger was never all he said he was; he had always been a bit of an enigma. Like his painting, one minute he was painting landscapes, then me and now abstract men. Somehow that was even worse. My Rodger had changed, and I had chosen not to notice.

Those last five minutes in the shed waiting for Shifty were the worst and they dragged on for what seemed an eternity.

Rodger started talking about leashes and marriage like he was Go Boy, "I know how he feels," he said "tied up and beaten about by a paper". *I mean what was he on about?*

I asked him and he snapped.

"Women, you're never happy, are you?" *I was confused.* "You never wanted me to paint you."

"Yes I did."

"No, you wanted me to make you look amazing."

I forgot about the sketches of me sleeping, the times he made me look, well, a bit past it, vulnerable.

"You wanted to control what I painted."

"That is not true."

"Well you're not happy with me painting a man. I knew you'd be against it."

I tried to tell him that was different, but he wasn't listening he had started to rant.

"What the hell does make you happy? I just can't figure you out and I am tired of trying. At least with a man you know where you are. With a man it's all out in the open, none of these... these... hidden bits. Everything is there for you to see."

"I can't help it if my bits are hidden," I snapped. "It's not my fault I don't have appendages swinging about the place for you to paint. Besides, I thought you liked a bit of mystery."

"Fuck mystery."

"I thought you were happy with your book shop and all that beige."

"Fucking beige. I am so sick of it and Jamie Oliver and that damn book shop and Mavis nicking all the toffees." He looked at me.

He was going to say more, I could see it on his lips. He was going to tell me how much he hated my belly dancing. Instead, he tossed his paintbrush into a bowl of water and stared out of the window again.

"Poor fucking dog trapped like that."

And then Jason (a testament to our education system) finally noticed that the dog was tied up and was actually barking for a reason. Jason decided to free Go Boy and Rodger watched.

"Go, Boy," he shouted, until Go Boy jumped over the fence and into our garden. Puss let out a cat-like shriek as the dog Go Boy landed outside the shed door, sending Puss into a frenzy of hissing and snarling, before making a few dashes at the dog's face.

Go Boy, dazed, fell against the shed door with a crash and pushed the door open. Bouncing back he circled around the hydrangeas, stopped to fertilise with a memento large enough to cover a serving plate and then ran...Rodger and I looked at each other; "no longer trapped," he said cryptically, and there was almost a smile on his face. I was just about to make a comment about an old dog and new tricks when my seductive music was abruptly turned off, followed by a loud bark, a yelp, a skidding noise and then a very loud 'fuck it' from Shifty.

"We're in the shed," yelled Rodger.

Finally after two days I got up from the bed. I needed tissues, coffee, or perhaps something stronger.

When Shifty walked in on us in the shed he started to laugh, and Shifty doesn't do laughing, *it's not really his best feature.* He laughed so hard he was clutching his stomach and crying and he has never cried, even at his father's funeral.

Being laughed at is not something new for me. I have been humiliated many times, but being laughed at when you're done up to seduce ripped my insides apart and I ran out. Like next door's dog before me, I couldn't get out of there quick enough and, as I tripped over my sandals and skidded on my scarves sprawled over the floor, Shifty finally stopped laughing, Rodger told him to, "shut up."

I looked out of the bedroom window and saw her, the Bag Lady, standing by the shed with its door swinging uselessly open. She was staring up at my window and, when she saw me, she let out a cackle.

I stared at her. I could imagine her tobacco scent, her face dark with months of grime, and then she waved and I waved back. It seemed that giving her a free coffee had gone to her head and now she wanted more.

"You coming out?" she yelled, and then started chanting about 'roads to despair', 'traffic lights and how mine was amber'. I was confused and amused especially when she began to dance, ruffling her skirt like a gypsy, adding a bit of soft shoe taps. She danced a jig like a girl, playful and full of fun and I couldn't help but watch.

Until that is, Rodger and Shifty arrived lugging DIY tools. I could hear them clattering about with bits of wood and talking about drills and roofing felt. Rodger had left one of his notes on the mirror; it was my turn to do the shop and I guess he assumed I was going.

Rodger had plans for the shed, I had seen them pinned on the kitchen notice board, cartoon-like drawings of paving, a pergola and more special sophisticated lighting – to, I now presume, capture the essence of man and push Rodger's testosterone-pumped abstracts to a higher level. I could even hear them talk in the garden about sweat lodges and liberation, a place for male bonding with I suspect the odd wire brush involved...

Shifty was laughing; "you should try it," he said to Rodger.

For two days I had been in bed crying my eyes out and there was Rodger making plans with not a thought for me.

The Bag Lady took off once she caught wind of Rodger and Shifty. She sprang to her feet like a young woman and started to run. I watched her skirt flap in the wind, as the whirl of a drill started right underneath my bedroom window.

How did she do it? How did she get up each day and play the same song to the same blank faces? Live so alone? I went downstairs, poured myself a strong coffee, did some serious makeup work on my puffy eyes and told myself that 'if she can find a reason to keep going, then why can't I?' Besides, who was going to make her coffee?

Chapter Twelve

THE INCOMER

One man's meat is another man's tofu.

The bookshop was hot, and the morning sun was streaming through the window. I looked out of the window into the empty street and felt a huge sense of relief. No customers to face, the gods had been kind.

I was a mixed ball of emotion. Just when I thought I had a grip on my situation and had gained some sort of control, Rodger had thrown me another curve ball, and confused me. I tried to tell myself I could work it out, that I was a self-taught, self-styled belly dancer who had brains as well as pliable hips, but I wasn't convinced. I had no idea what to do.

I decided to bask in the sunlight for a bit and absorb the energies of the day, a favourite expression of Imogen's. I sat on the couch, and began my first intake of cleansing breaths.

The Read and be Thankful was, at the beginning, Rodger's baby; his vision, his idea of a fresh venture for us to build together. Rodger wanted a new life, and as he said, *The Read and be Thankful* was our chance to contemplate, read and be thankful. Not that he appeared to be thankful now; he was about as thankful as I was fertile and ready to reproduce. I was confused; had he changed or had I just never listened?

At the beginning, I helped him with what to put in the shop and looking back I now remember the arguments. "Women want earthy, womanly things; books on dancing, self-help, and anything to do with cooking," I said.

He called me narrow-minded; "not all women are like you," he said. At the time I thought he was paying me a compliment, now I am beginning to wonder.

I looked about the shop. The new Rodger's presence was everywhere, despite the bowl of free toffees. I had closed my eyes, turned away and lied to myself. Perhaps I was still living on past memories, hoping that one day things would return to the way they used to be.

The bookshop had become all matey, macho man on full throttle. The free toffees were now served with potent cough drops for fishermen. Nigella Lawson, my chocolate loving icon, is now shelved at the back of the shop, giving way to Rick Stein and his fish. And the dance section is nothing but a distant memory. The books have been either tossed into the half-price bucket like washing in a laundry basket or given, donated, dumped at Mary's *Meals On Wheels* shop around the corner. And she is selling them for ten pence or five for forty pence. My goddess books, my mysteries of the harem novels... you name it, it was there. My books were outside the second-hand shop on an old rickety table like unwanted, dusty house plants that someone had tired of watering.

And the beige walls, which were once covered in posters at my insistence of great Scottish women, are now covered in posters of sheds owned by very famous men, not to mention the accompanying calendars, and postcards, all along the same theme. There is even a collection of pens on sale with pictures of a shed on them; and, depending on which way you move the pen, the door opens and a man appears holding a set of hedge cutters. Who is that for? Someone with a fetish for sheds or hedge cutters?

And there is a whole section of books on sheds. I did once ask Rodger, when he was designing what he called the *'new look' Read and be Thankful* if there was a market for such things and he told me that there were plenty of men out there like him. But I never listened. I guess I should have. I mean, as Kay pointed out to me, what is the point of you asking a question if you don't stick around for the answer? Guess I should have listened to her as well.

However, the macho man bookshop was all I had and as Mavis often says "sometimes you just have to get on with it".

So I continued to stare into the empty street until the Bag Lady came into view. She waved at me, crossed the street, and plonked herself by the shop doorway. I watched her set out her blanket, and unpack her organ. She then knocked on the door and handed me her plug; apparently the batteries had died and the Co-op had *run out*.

As if...could they not just have been honest and told her to go away? I know she is not everyone's flavour of the month but she isn't stupid. I mean you are talking about a woman who has captured the imagination of a whole town. Her rendition of *Come on Eileen* can be heard from just about any corner of Lochgilphead. Everyone is singing it. Even the Co-op started playing pan-piped versions of Dexy's Midnight Runners songs. And this woman stopped the Gala day, with a couple of geese and some swans.

She deserved, at least, a little honesty.

It was easy to find her batteries, just as it was easy to make her coffee. In fact I took great comfort in hearing her tune up and play her one and only song. By the end of the day I had found a decent set of ear plugs. Thanks to her I wasn't bothered once by anyone and my facing the world had been easier for it and well worth the half of jar of Nescafé I went through.

I went home with a plan for the next day; not just coffee, but some hot chocolate and maybe some soup. I was going to make it all myself and through the day when I had had enough of her singing I was going to silence her with food so hot that it would take her ages to eat.

It took me a whole week and more before I could face Rodger again, before I didn't exit as he entered. A week cooking for the Bag Lady and flicking through those self-help books I never noticed before. On the Friday night, as I was making my end of the week frothy cappuccino, Rodger walked in and for the first time I didn't run out. I decided to stay, to look him in the eye and get it over with.

I watched him microwave his coffee and spoon three sugars into it and waited as he began to tell me that the Bag Lady was a "curse on the shop". *As if a woman with one pair of shoes could be a curse.*

"Why is she sitting outside my shop?" he said.

I told him about the batteries. Rodger clutched his espresso. "You know she only goes there when you're there." He looked at me hard. "You're encouraging her, aren't you?"

I didn't say anything.

"Because if you are, you can just un-encourage her. I mean, I was walking by the other morning, whole goddamn street was full of kids, looking for her it was like some Charles Dickens movie."

Of course Rodger's idea of a street full of kids is a couple, who have taken to giving her rolls, on their way to school, hardly Charles Dickens, but I didn't say that. I could see the strain on Rodger's face; apparently his painting was at a crucial point.

"Shifty says she'll move eventually, but when?"

I didn't answer but watched as he drained his coffee cup, stood up and headed for the shed. "You'll have to go in tomorrow," he said. "I just can't cope with her, not now at this late stage of my work."

I didn't argue or, for that matter, ask about his painting. I welcome the Bag Lady, the woman of muddy tartan. She seemed to attract a different type of audience and making the shop Rodger-less was a complete bonus. As I said to the girls, any woman who could instigate the destruction of a Zumba extravagance was welcome, no matter what state her personal hygiene was in. And the fact that she annoyed Rodger was better than whipped cream. I still felt humiliated.

Chapter Thirteen

THE VAN

A Transit van by any other name is still difficult to turn.

I was sitting in *The Read and be Thankful* browsing my latest *Single is Great* read when I heard a noise from the street. I looked up; I couldn't believe it. Rodger was out of his shed, out of Ardrishaig and running across the street shouting, while clutching a pile of packaging.

"You can take this back," he said. "This is no more a sweat lodge than I am a coke can."

I have never known my Rodger to shout and run in public, even in the days of belly dancing when a few of the old ones in the audience fell asleep, and there he was running alongside a van with his precious pal Shifty trying to stop him. Rodger's face was as red as the day Blondie took the takings. Then, just as I was about to top up my morning espresso, there was a crash, loud enough to make me drop my cup. I rammed on my shoes – I always think better barefooted – and raced out to the street. By the time I got there, there was a lot of shouting and the Bag Lady had been told to 'shut it!'

The white van had stopped, leaving a trail of skid marks, smashed street signs and a window box behind it, while Rodger was lying prostrate under some bubble wrap and cardboard. All there was to see of him was an outstretched hand and his battered face turned towards *The Read and be Thankful*.

"He just ran out like a mad man," said the van driver. "Right in front of me. I told him I don't do returns, but would he listen?"

Rodger's fingers twitched as he glared at the driver. "Take it back," he said, through gritted teeth.

The driver looked at him. "I told you I only deliver, mate. You need to go to the post office for returns."

"I said; take it back, the gay stuff, my paintings are for every man..."

Shifty was wringing his hands and looking nothing like the super-confident man behind the bar. "It's my fault," he said. "I encouraged him to take the assertiveness classes and now look at him, butched up like a pit bull terrier. He took one look at the flat pack and blew a fuse."

I guess that's what being celibate does to a man.

I spent the rest of the day sitting by a hospital bed, clutching a plastic cup of dark liquid feeling like an extra out of *Mash*, as some dark-haired man who looked nothing like Alan Alda walked in and out, mumbling on about X-rays and poking Rodger about in a manner that made me feel invisible.

Shifty sat next to me. He was completely useless, I even had to do all the coffee fetching and when the non-Alda nurse who kept appearing from nowhere began to talk about reconstruction, Shifty nearly fainted. It took three shots of Nescafé gold along with the whiff of a day-old tuna roll, to bring him around.

"Reconstruction at his age could be a positive thing," said the nurse flatly.

"I doubt it," Shifty muttered.

I reassured Shifty that reconstruction of a toe was not a big operation and preferable to having it removed. And Shifty said nothing.

"Now," said the nurse. "You're to sign here, here and here."

"Whatever for?" Shifty asked.

"Permission to do whatever is necessary," he said, with a poor impression of intimidation.

Not really wanting to know what the *whatever* was, we watched as Rodger scribbled his name and then collapsed from the effort, after which I signed and then the nurse took the form away.

"I should have stopped him going to those assertiveness classes," Shifty said. "Discovering the man within was too much too soon, he wasn't ready." Shifty sighed and tossed his half-drunk coffee at the bin, a little of it splattering onto the wall behind the bin.

"He really let that driver have it," muttered Shifty.

Rodger went for the driver?

I looked at my Rodger's corduroy trousers, cut and hanging down the side of the bed like a used tissue. Rodger, who had never had a day's illness, was spread out before me like a piece of meat on a supermarket trolley. Since when had he cared about delivery men?

"If only he hadn't driven over the hydrangeas. Rodger was using them for his new piece, a collage of petals," said Shifty. "The driver said he didn't see the hydrangeas and when Rodger made a scene he, the driver, called him a fanny."

"No one's ever called him a fanny before," I said.

Shifty looked at me. "You're not taking this seriously, are you?"

"What do you mean?"

"You don't understand, do you? If you did you wouldn't have made such a song and dance about the shed in the first place."

"What?"

"His paintings mean everything to him."

I looked at Rodger's now limp moustache, lying flat against his skin. I could almost remember the feel of it against me. He never used to be so volatile. The Rodger I knew was as laid back as Puss after chicken. The Rodger I knew loved mornings. Watching me rise from the bed, throw on a robe, and making me breakfasts were all acts of erotic pleasure for him, especially creating his cappuccino. He always had a thing for froth.

Now according to Shifty he was enraged because some van driver who he would never see again called his art porn...for men.

"I don't know what has got into him," said Shifty, as he turned to Rodger and in an extra loud voice told him to "chill."

"I just wanted him to take it back," Rodger muttered through clenched teeth.

I went to touch his hand, but he pulled it away and then grimaced in pain. None of us saw the nurse return, still clutching his folder.

"What sort of name is this?" he snapped, pointing to my signature.

"It's my name," I said.

"Funny kind of name, was your mum on something?"

I looked at him. I had been through a lot that morning. I had supplied Shifty with endless cups of black stuff, none of which he'd paid for, while putting up with his drivel about the Bag Lady, as well as calling me flippant. And I still had a delivery, to unpack and price, along with my second and most important espresso that would now be forming some sort of black rim about my favourite mug. And now I was having the nurse take the piss out of my name. How much can a woman take? I drew myself up to my five-two stance, and met his glare.

"He gave it to me," I said gesturing to Rodger.

Rodger grunted.

"A long time ago, before you were old enough to pull a syringe, and I have been using it ever since."

The nurse looked at me like I was speaking Japanese.

"She's a belly dancer," sighed Shifty.

Unimpressed, the nurse looked at his clipboard, looked at his watch and mumbled something under his breath. He then walked off as Rodger, rallying the last of his energy, shouted, "She's not my wife."

The nurse didn't hear.

Rodger began to groan in pain... which is what comes from playing with a shed early in the morning without a decent bacon roll inside you. He pulled Shifty closer to him. "Where am I?" he muttered.

Before I could say A&E, the curtains swished open and another nurse entered in green scrubs. "He's all prepped and ready to rock and roll," he said, flashing what looked like a new set of dentures. "Now you'll have to let us do what we do best."

"You're not going anywhere near his..." I motioned vaguely to his lower body.

Shifty flashed me a look.

"It's his foot and his jaw that is broken..." he looked at his clip-board "...err, Nefertiti. His shoulder is a bit bruised and his hip, well, that's just arthritis." He flashed his teeth at me again, said, "no other bits mentioned," and swished the curtain apart to allow the porter in.

I watched as *nurse-joker* and the porter wheeled Rodger away like last night's takeaway. I wanted to shout *change him back; make him like he used to be.* But I didn't. I was now on my own, with an empty cup in my hand and half a chocolate bar in my bag. Not much to console myself with...

Shifty had left. He followed behind Rodger's trolley, mumbling something about 'car trouble and clients', and told me I would need to find my own way home.

So I caught the bus back to Lochgilphead. I'd like to say it was me keeping a keen eye on my carbon footprint. But the truth was, I did not want to stay in Glasgow.

The last time I stayed in Glasgow it was in a dubious B&B. I remember walking into the '70s reception area and wondering if a 'two nights for the price of one' deal was really such a good idea. It stank of sausages, fulfilling the promise of a mediocre breakfast, and the poker-faced receptionist barely spoke even after five decent jokes.

When I arrived at the bus station the Campbeltown bus was already parked with its engine running and a queue that had me panicking. I joined the queue and prayed that no one would recognise me. Not an easy thing to do on the Campbeltown bus, where everyone knows everyone. I wanted to be left alone, I had had enough.

I stared at the ground and wondered just how long it would take to actually get on the bus. And if, once on the bus, I would be able to sleep. The last thing I wanted was to be stuck next to some familiar face talking about the price of fish in the shop.

"If you're not booked, get to the back of the queue," shouted the bus driver from his seat. He shouted so loud that a pensioner, who was already on the bus but was moving annoyingly slowly to her seat, dropped her shopping. "Sit down or you're off the bus," he barked. "And no hot food."

I watched from the back of the 'not booked queue', clutching my coffee. I was ready for Mr Hitler; my latté was lidded and I was not going to waste my £1.59 just to please him. I braced myself as I was finally motioned by the driver to step onto the bus. He contemptuously eyed my hot drink. I had my retort ready and was just about to use it when he shouted so loudly at those behind me I nearly dropped my cup.

"No hot drinks on the bus without a lid. Has that got a lid? Does that look like a lid? Don't look like a lid to me! What? No, no, no, sunshine... You'll need to drink it, and we'll be leaving in five with or without you!"

He flashed a look at me as if I was his comrade. "Look at her, she's got a lid. Why can't you have a lid? Unbelievable!"

So much for incognito! I walked onto the bus with all eyes burning into me, half of whom I knew.

"How's Rodger?" said one of his customers from the seat behind and pretty soon regretted asking.

"He was knocked over by a van," I said, "all because he was called a fanny."

"No; your Rodger?"

"Well I wouldn't call him mine anymore but yes..."

The woman nodded, sage-like, as I moved beside her and began to talk about my day from hell; a day when I was let down by some stupid barman not giving me a lift back; a day when my Rodger refused to hold my hand when about to go into surgery.

"And that's where I left him comatose and dribbling, like a teething baby... and nothing like the man I had fallen out with," I said, I looked around and she was asleep, in fact the whole bus was dozing, apart from the driver.

I stared out of the window and thought about the past. Years ago when I was in Glasgow, alone and single, was that worse? A day when I had to sit squashed up by the bus window breathing the fumes of someone who thought body odour, if left, matured like wine. I stared into the eight pm blackness outside the bus window. All those feelings of being rejected came back...

In another life I was known as Janice, a student belly dancer who was ignored and undesired. Like old Mav, my pelvis, my womanhood, lay dormant, outcast and unused as I cleaned tables in my ex-husband's café and cooked him meals he did not want. I was a woman wishing her life away and, like Mavis, I thought belly dancing was the answer.

We lived in Norwich and wanted children, but they never appeared. I thought we wanted the same things. Until one day, I walked into the café and bent over a table was my husband like a dog on heat and her screaming like a banshee, with her chipped stiletto heels pointing at the sky. And that was that!

Twenty-one years of marriage wiped away with just one glance of my husband's naked pimply flesh pulsating to *Relax* by Frankie Goes To Hollywood.

I remember sitting in our lounge room, staring at his Christmas presents waiting to be wrapped. On the table was the Christmas tree, candles and Christmas cards from some of the customers. I looked at his empty chair, the newly acquired second-hand chair that he sat on every night flicking his cigarette ash everywhere but in an ashtray, and wondered why it had taken me so long.

It wasn't the first time I had thought about leaving, but venturing into the unknown scared me senseless. Now I had no choice. The stiletto heel-wearer had done me a favour, although I would never thank her for it; she had taken what I had lost already and pushed me to go. I had no option, I couldn't stay and compete. I had nothing to fight with. Like my old granddad used to say, "Never stay where the pencil does not fit." So with my coin belt and Hassam Ramzy CDs, I moped my way to Scotland, as far from the stiletto heel-wearer as possible.

And now here I was again in Glasgow, thinking about another possible ex. The next ex... This time there was no stiletto wearer, just a pile of paintings and a man who no longer wanted to watch me dance. Maybe after his operation he might change. Who knows, but as long as there were no stilettos involved, I told myself there was always a chance.

I woke up in Ardrishaig. My mouth was dry, my coffee was on the floor, and my neck was stiff. My fellow passenger was long gone, leaving little more than a faint whiff of body odour. But I had no time to rub, complain or smell. I had just enough time to grab my bag and get off before the driver started to shout again.

Standing in the rain watching the bus leave, I realised I was going home to an empty house. There was no fire, no 'how was your day?' and now not even a light on in the shed, just Puss at the front door waiting to be fed and I had run out of chicken.

Chapter Fourteen

THE JOURNEY

The truth is out there but who wants to see it.

Shifty and I were heading to Glasgow to visit Rodger. We were on our own and, as always, not on good terms. The next day after Rodger's accident I had woken dazed and confused, wondering whether I should see Rodger, I wanted to; I wanted to be the good woman, and hold his hand. But as the hospital said, he would be out in a few days and as Sheryl pointed out, "does he want you there, let alone holding his hand?"

However, Shifty called, he was heading to Glasgow to visit Rodger and he wanted to "grab a few things." And I stupidly agreed. Shifty came in the back door looking like this was the last place he wanted to be and I offered him a coffee. And then he started to ask about toothbrushes and sponge bags, which got right up my nose.

"If anyone is taking his toothbrush," I said, "don't you think it should be me?" Part of me felt that there was still a chance. Rodger was in hospital, angry and hurt, maybe thinking about us and our past might change his mind. After all he hadn't actually told me we were finished.

Shifty didn't argue; instead he said that I should speak to Rodger, ask him who he would like to bring his toothbrush and then, as I pointed out he couldn't speak as his jaw would be wired, Shifty shrugged his shoulders and said, "perhaps you should ask in person."

Maybe he felt for me and my loss. I mean, I saw Rodger and me growing old together, sitting on a veranda with a homebrew. I pictured us together, like cheese and chutney, together until the end, looking over my scrapbooks of performances, maybe even writing my memoirs. I mean, I had all the photos and clippings in boxes.

"Not much room for his art work in that plan," said Shifty.

And I blushed; was I a little self-absorbed as Kay often said? I had assumed Rodger wanted what I wanted.

"You should ask him what he wants," continued Shifty, "it would make things a lot easier."

It takes around two hours to get from Lochgilphead to Glasgow and in that time Shifty's moods swung from chatty to thoughtful musing.

I had known Shifty for years, and yet now as I sat next to him in his pale blue Fiat listening to him philosophise like someone on Big Brother, I realised I didn't know him at all. He was like a stranger to me, especially when he began to talk about "letting go" and how "all things come to an end".

Frankly, I wanted to tell him to shut up. It was bad enough sitting next to a frustrated rally driver and wondering if the next corner was going to be my last, but to listen to Shifty's half-baked philosophies was enough to make you want to stop breathing.

Then, from out of nowhere, as though he had just remembered something, he started muttering about his ex-wife and her preference for leather over nylon.

"What?" I said, jolting awake.

Shifty started to talk about how his ex-wife had changed and how he chose not to notice. How she tried to talk and how he chose to ignore, "all the signs were there" he said, without one mention of Ardennes. "But I wasn't listening."

"Oh, I see," I said.

"She was a woman of taste," mused Shifty, "a woman who preferred sitting in to takeaway."

I had no idea what he was talking about, and asked.

"Well she was the sort of woman who liked fillet steak in a restaurant and expensive wine. I am more a fish and chips, and coke man. I was trying to run a business while she was trying to ...well." Shifty's voice drifted off.

It was on the tip of my tongue to say 'belly dance and whatever with Ardennes' but I held back. I started to think about the time when Shifty's wife left him, and how much Shifty hated Ardennes and how much hurt there was on Shifty's face. For the first time I looked back and felt a little ashamed at my behaviour; Sheryl called me thoughtless.

A few days after Shifty's wife left him I was in the Argyll with the girls and he was not in the best of trim. I told him 'not to take his ex's departure personally'.

"Oh, how should I take it?" he snapped, shoving a glass under the vodka optics with extra force. "My woman has dumped me for a male model and you tell me not to take it personally. No wonder your Rodger looks pissed off half the time."

Sheryl warned me, told me to keep quiet, but I continued.

I told Shifty that he was lucky he had a business to keep him busy and that at least it was now out in the open, "So she preferred the pelvic action of the Spanish kind," I said. "You'll do better."

Shifty took my glass which I hadn't finished and began to wash it, all the while telling me not to 'mention him or his goddamn pelvis in my bar; that man was my friend'.

We left soon after that, probably because Shifty refused to serve me, and as Kay drove me home she called me among other things brutal and insensitive, and Sheryl didn't say a word.

Now as I looked at Shifty's profile I understood why. I watched as he negotiated the Balloch roundabout, where a queue of cars was forming. I felt sad, I thought of the pain I had experienced in the last few weeks; *what must have he felt?*

We were at the back of a long queue into Glasgow and when Shifty suggested a McDonald's I agreed, even though I hate the place.

❄

Shifty leaned towards me over a bright orange table while clutching his Americano coffee. It was almost finished but he, it seemed, wasn't, he was ruminating about the past, and how everything was in the past, "I never think of her now," he said. "Everything has a shelf life."

Shifty had plonked an all-day breakfast wrap in front of me and one in front of him. He demolished his and then when I picked at mine began to talk about "break ups". Shifty looked at me with his piercing green eyes. I never noticed before exactly how green they were, although he did have a green jumper on. He is a handsome man if you're into fast-driving blonds and for a moment I could see why his wife had married him.

Then he mumbled something about how, "We all have to move on sometimes, including me," and I got a pretty good picture as to why she left. He was telling me it was over and I should accept it, who was he to tell me that?

"We all have a shelf life," he said.

"That's what Rodger says," I said.

"And it is best to end as friends," continued Shifty.

"He says that as well, usually when he's claiming something which I have bought, and he now wants, like most of the kitchen."

"Well, he is a decent cook," said Shifty.

I muttered something about how I had forgotten, as it had been so long. Shifty's face softened as he looked out of the window with a reflective expression. He then fumbled in his pocket, pulled a notebook from it and pushed it across to me. "Have a look," he said "I wrote these when I was in love with her and now, well, you'll see, maybe it will help you."

I told him I wasn't into poetry but he insisted; "go on," he said. "I don't mind, in the past and all that." He opened the notebook onto a page in the middle of the notebook and told me to read from the top. His handwriting was not easy to read. He had written in black capital letters on an old menu which had been stapled to the notepad and folded up into a tiny square. I pressed the paper out and began to read.

It was a poem about pizza, a love poem, I ask you. I read the first line and pretended to read the rest...not easy when the writer is staring at you from across the table waiting for a reaction.

"There was a time," said Shifty, "when I thought I was a poet."

I looked at the last line where he talked about his woman being the "butter on his corn". The poem was ridiculous, *proof that when sex turns to love making, the brain actually stops functioning.*

"I nearly sent them into the *Fyne News*," said Shifty wistfully.

"It was probably a good idea you didn't. I mean, I don't think you should give up pulling pints just yet," I said.

Shifty was silent.

Then I told him that he was a better barman than a poet.

And he still said nothing.

"Your potential," I said, with my best intellectual voice, "is not obvious... as yet." *I was trying to be gentle.*

Shifty, remaining silent, pulled the notebook from me. "What would you know about poetry anyway? Belly dancer, you're just a tough old bird like the rest."

Me, like the rest? I am unique.

"You just have to take the piss, don't you?" he snapped.

Here we go...

"You just can't help yourself, can you?"

I knew he'd start...

"I just thought," he said, "that if I told you how much my wife had meant to me, how much I loved her... Well, now it's over, and I'm over it. Then well... so can you be over it, I mean. Move on, so to speak. When you meet Rodger and..."

"What would you know about my Rodger just because you built a shed together?"

"Oh, fuck it, never mind. Forget it, I was only trying to help."

"Trying to help me! Before I got into your car, you were asking me for petrol money."

"Suit yourself," he said, and began to clear the table; he chucked my half eaten breakfast wrap in the bin followed by my coffee. "If you want to walk into that hospital thinking that you and Rodger have a chance then go right ahead, but don't say I didn't try and help."

Shifty, as I said, blew hot and cold, one minute he would be putting up posters for my goddess workshop, *trying to help,* and then next barring me from the pub. As if I was going to take advice from him. I remember when his wife left; he went through a whole host of emotions, sometimes as venomous as a red-back spider. Shifty not only whinged about her for months, but made it impossible for her to stay in the area, and then he sulked forever. In fact, it is only in the past few months that Shifty seemed to have perked up or as Kay liked to say, "Regained his gay old ways."

Now here he was giving me advice about moving on.

When we arrived at the hospital Shifty told me to go ahead. He said he had a phone call to make and that perhaps it would be best if I saw Rodger by myself!

Chapter Fifteen

THE HOSPITAL

When in doubt hide it under a mat and hope the mice eat it.

I walked into Rodger's hospital room revved up on McDonald's coffee and disillusioned by Shifty's philosophy. The ward had been modernised, and all the walls had windows; from one room you could see into the corridor, and across to the other rooms opposite. You could see who was stumbling to the toilet, the nurses casually walking around looking more like cleaners than nurses, and doctors looking too young to be doctors and worryingly tired.

This was my golden opportunity to prove him wrong, that splitting up was not such a great idea. Somehow, the idea of him in hospital as helpless as a beached whale made it seem possible.

I heard music playing from the next ward, the start of *Days of our Lives*. It echoed through the passageway like a premonition.

I stood in the corridor and a memory came back of the Bag Lady. At the time I thought it was the ramblings of a woman malnourished, but as I remembered it my intuition started to rumble.

I looked into her grey eyes. The whites were pure and the lashes still long; in a time gone by those eyes would have been beautiful.

"Like sand in the hourglass, so are the men in our lives," she said.

Rodger shared a room with Mr Sharp, an elderly man with a lopsided face and a mass of grey hair spread like a fan on his pillow.

Sitting beside him was Mrs Sharp, an equally elderly woman with little hair and an impressive set of dentures, and Mr Sharp Junior, a man who looked like he had recently retired and was living well on it.

Rodger was not, as I imagined, trussed up like a turkey in a hammock, but sitting with his broken foot on a stool and his mouth clenched tight. I stared at him. His jaw was wired, his hair had slicked back and for the first time his caterpillar eyebrows were on full view. His eyes were shut and nothing moved on his face.

"He's asleep," shouted Mrs Sharp.

Like I hadn't worked that out for myself.

I put my hand tentatively beside my use-to-be soul mate. I watched and wondered when his shoulders would move again, when his lips would smile again, and if he would ever swing his legs from my bed with the gay abandonment of a man after an encounter. Then he woke up, saw me and looked disappointed, which was soon followed by an expression of pity.

Rodger's reaction hit me to the core of my bones, and I wasn't too keen to explore why. I come from generations who made it through the Blitz, who knew when truth was best swept under the carpet, and right now, that was how I felt; keep it under the carpet for as long as possible.

"Once the truth is out you can't put it back," my mother used to say, "so think before you ask." My mother was a woman of many lives, a woman who cleaned like a demon but was not particular about the men who visited. She was never keen on questions and right now neither was I.

Rodger's face said a thousand things to me. None made me feel good and a lot made me feel like I shouldn't have come. And as for my intuition, I wanted to sweep that under the carpet too.

"Shifty here yet?" said Mrs Sharp. "Nice man, that Shifty, brought in something for himself to eat." She gestured to her husband. I could see Mr Sharp and his son look at my empty hands, with a 'did you bring anything?' look.

According to the Sharps, on the night of the accident Shifty came back to the hospital after I left, and stayed by Rodger's bed until he was conscious. And then went out, brought in food and fed the Sharps despite Rodger still being asleep. My stomach lurched at the thought. I felt a prick at my heart, a knot in my stomach; *Shifty?*

Rodger grunted. I pulled a Mars bar from my bag and offered him a bite. He closed his eyes, with a head-turning no thanks. I attempted a joke about the hospital food, *one time Rodger would have chuckled to sleep on that one!* The Sharps called it poor taste, "he just had his jaw wired," and Mr Sharp said, "what you playing at?"

I looked at him; he raised his thick eyebrows with a sigh and turned away.

Visiting someone in a hospital isn't the easiest thing to do; it's the talking, it's so wearing. It's like sex outside, very uncomfortable and there is always the possibility of an audience. For a start, there are the nurses walking in and out like they own the place. And then there are the other visitors staring at the TV, watching programmes they hate while trying to avoid eye contact with other visitors. It's like being on the Underground.

However, sitting in a ward beside your ex who can't speak and knowing that he would rather someone else was sitting in your place, and knowing that everyone else in the room also knows, is not only uncomfortable, but incredibly painful. I looked around the room, it's never easy to realise you're the last one to know, when in truth you should be the first.

Mr Sharp started to talk about his breakfast, fried eggs and sausage, and no one listened; the son and wife were busy talking to each other. Then Mr Sharp started to shout about his sausages until his wife told him to calm down, and that he was in a hospital and not a cruise ship.

"I brought in a magazine for you," I said. "You want me to read it to you?"

Rodger grunted no.

"Not even the problems page?"

Rodger shook his head.

Mr Sharp was now fixated on sausages specifically grilled ones, and Mrs Sharp through gritted teeth was telling him to be quiet. Mr Sharp Junior tried to calm his father, who by now had decided to get out of bed and visit the kitchen and see to the sausages himself.

I could hear two children racing in the corridor, shouting at each other followed by a push and then a whimper; I looked up to watch them and saw Shifty in the corridor. Rodger did too and his face, well, his eyebrows spelt happiness while a lump made its presence felt in my throat.

"Hey, mate, how you doing?" said Shifty.

Shifty looked handsome, gentle and completely different; I watched him hand a roll and sausage to Mr Sharp, who sat down on his chair with a smile. Shifty pulled up a chair on Rodger's other side and asked him if he was hungry. Rodger's eyes gestured to me, and there was enough eye contact between Rodger and Shifty to make even a rational person like me feel paranoid.

My heart began to beat against my chest. Why did I allow myself to do this?

An elderly man shuffled up to the doorway. He looked lost, confused and frail. "I'm needing a pee," he said. "And I can't find Rex, he's missing. How will I get the sheep in?"

The nurse shouted at him from down the corridor and the old man, along with most of the visitors, jolted with fright. "The toilets are the other way, Mr McKenzie, you'll frighten the children!"

Mr Sharp Senior, mumbling something about 'no need to shout', got up from his chair.

"I said you're going the wrong way, Mr McKenzie," shouted the nurse. Mr Sharp gave her the finger.

The two children were still racing around in the corridor, as Mr McKenzie tried to master his Zimmer with shaky hands and rhythmic shuffling.

He and Mr Sharp almost made it to the toilet, until the two children circled about them once too often. Mr McKenzie panicked, lost confidence and crashed to the floor, leaving a trail of tissue and pyjamas behind him. The two children disappeared like dandelion seeds in the wind, while Mr Sharp tried to help Mr McKenzie by dragging at his arm and calling him 'ole boy'.

"Mr Sharp," shouted the nurse. "How many times have I told you to leave the other patients alone?"

"Hear, hear," muttered Mrs Sharp.

"Go on back to your room; I said, go back to your room."

Mr Sharp, undaunted, marched back to the ward like a war veteran. "That's the Alzheimer's," he shouted. "The home help says it's like wildfire, everyone's got it. Haven't they, son?"

And that's when it happened. Rodger took Shifty's hand as they looked into each other's eyes and laughed, like lovers with their own secret world. The truth was out, and I could no longer pretend. In one moment, my whole world shifted and the carpet could no longer hide the truth. There was a stiletto wearer after all and it was Shifty.

I had to get out quick, I felt like I was choking...

I stood in the ladies telling myself to keep it real, but I started to feel sick and sweaty. My stomach began to rotate like a washing machine on spin, churning the McDonalds filter around. I was alone, rejected again. How did this happen?

My stomach squeezed so tight I could hardly breathe. I felt scared. Cars were driving by. I could hear them at the window, people were shouting and laughing; outside the world was going on, and yet I felt paralysed. I could hardly breathe and I wondered if I would live to finish the chocolates I had left on the corduroy couch.

I sat down on the top of the bog like a woman in labour, breathless, sweaty and flushed. My heart felt like it was banging on my rib cage, ready to explode. For the first time in my life I felt like I was going to die. I felt as if my chest was going to explode all over the toilet. And I would be found on the floor with all my innards splashed across the 'safe sex' poster.

Maybe Kay was right; maybe I did need a quack, after all.

Chapter Sixteen

A BOX OF RED

Women expect too much from a haircut.

When down, we women head to the hairdressers with a 'cut it all off, make me blonde now' demand, or at least splash out in Boots. So, after the hospital visit from hell, I bought hair dye from the pound shop and cut myself a fringe while Puss stood in the doorway of the bathroom watching.

To be rejected by someone you put up with is bad enough; to be rejected when you are in love is painful beyond words. However, for a woman to lose her man to another man, the pain is indefinable, although humiliation and confusion do come close; especially when your man at one time, seemed inspired by a woman's body, *mine that is.*

When Rodger first wanted to paint me I couldn't believe it. No one had looked at me for years. I had not long been belly dancing and was still getting used to the feeling of celebrating my own body when Rodger came along. He made me feel beautiful, like a goddess, and he wanted to paint me in all shades, emotions and sizes. Now, thanks to Shifty, he has tossed me aside like a used condom; dumped me for a grumpy barman, built like a rugby player. There was no hope left.

Hiding the grey was all I could muster and a week later I was still at that grey stage.

Each morning I woke up with Puss on my stomach, while I stared at the chandelier suspended from the bedroom ceiling and all the purple scarves billowing around it. The bedroom was the first room we decorated in our then favourite colour, purple; now I hated the damn colour and the damn chandelier especially when Rodger hung notes on it.

Recovering from the hospital visit wasn't easy; that night I found Rodger's stash of nettle whisky, looked at it and then ate chocolate instead – not that that helped either. Watching everyone treat Rodger and Shifty as a couple rather than Rodger and me hurt. When I saw the nurses call Shifty to the nurses' station and talk with the doctors, I knew they were a couple and I was invisible, dispensed with, and no longer necessary.

I mean, why Shifty? Okay, he looks good in jeans and can tuck his shirt in and get away with it, but he is so manly, and he dances like an ape on hot coals. I saw him at the last Christmas *do*, his hips are about as pliable as a slab of cement. Shifty has as much rhythm as an inflatable ball. His idea of dancing is jumping up and down to the Pogues like a kid on a trampoline.

How could Rodger, a man who swept me off my feet with a love for my dance, choose him over me?

I must have sat in that toilet for ages trying to get it together as women went in and out of the next cubicle. I watched the change of shoes at the space between the floor and the wall separating the two cubicles and wondered if anyone would care for me again. And when I got tired of that I stared at the wall which hadn't seen paint in years and was peeling off like a bad case of sunburn.

All I have is Puss, a cat with an extraordinarily long tail, a cat who sees herself as Rodger's. Rodger brought her home one day and she has never seemed to have forgotten it. She sits outside the shed waiting for him to let her in, but thanks to Shifty's cat allergy he no longer does. So eventually, when Rodger shoos her away she spends her time staring into the garden at the kitchen window or waiting at the back door willing Rodger to come in while turning her nose up at every tin I open.

If I was honest, I have to admit that the signs were there. There were times when Rodger tried to tell me, Shifty even tried in the car, but I didn't want to know; if I didn't hear it, it wasn't happening and there was a chance. Now there is no turning back, no chance, just who gets what in our redundant home.

It took me a week to even contemplate the humiliation; being stuck in a hospital toilet having panic attacks was bad enough, but worse was working out how to escape with dignity. Finally after using half a roll of toilet paper for my tears a nurse came and banged on the toilet door. She didn't even ask if I was okay, only said that the cleaner needed to get in so could I hurry up and finish what it was I was trying to do.

I had stupidly left my bag in the car and had to go back into the ward where they were still holding hands. I walked in to find the curtain was pulled around Rodger's bed and I could hear grunts and Shifty talking in hushed tones along the lines of 'does she know?' and 'who should tell her?' and 'you'd think she'd get the picture by now.'

"She can hear," said Mr Sharp.

Mr Sharp Junior looked uncomfortable as Mrs Sharp berated her husband for poking his nose into other folks' business.

"I tried to tell her in the car," said Shifty, "but all she wanted to do was play CDs. How did you put up with her for so long?"

I sat down with an uncomfortable smile at the Sharps.

"All that belly dancing stuff does my head in."

Mr Sharp Junior smiled awkwardly back at me.

"A woman her age…" *That hurt!* "And she laughed at my poem".

Rodger mumbled through his wired jaw a string of garbled words, what I heard was "Told you *pause* viper." *Viper, I assumed, meant me.*

"I said, she can hear," shouted Mr Sharp, with a spray of his sausage roll.

As I walked out I shouted to Shifty that I would wait by the car and left as Mr and Mrs Sharp's voice echoed through the corridors… *"Will you stop shouting?" "But she was sitting right here, she could hear every-thing." "And you're making it worse, stupid old goat!"*

❄

Puss stretched out on my body like a lizard in the sun. She purred and for a minute looked at me with sleepy eyes. I wondered how soon she would forget about Rodger, and was just about to go for a small stroke when I heard yelling from outside my bedroom window. The same yelling that woke me every morning since I let her sit at the shop doorway. I stuck my head out the window and like every other morning she yelled.

"You coming out?" she shouted. I think she has become addicted to my coffee.

Since the Bag Lady had taken up residence in the shop doorway, she had begun to wheedle her way into my life and, despite Kay and Sheryl's warnings, I wasn't putting up a fight. Sheryl said I was vulnerable, Kay called it gullible, and even Mavis, despite her domestic bliss, warned me yesterday about that goose lady and the need for restraint. "You should let the Social deal with her," she said.

But I liked being woken up in the morning and liked her in my garden. As I told the girls, you couldn't smell her from the bedroom. Every morning she would yell, I would wave and then she would disappear only to reappear when I was at the shop, door opened and her cappuccino almost made.

And her repertoire has expanded. I think it has something to do with her electric organ and a poor battery charger; because sometimes she brings a small hand drum instead of her organ. The drum has really taken her entertainment to new heights.

This morning she had a different song, a new song, a song with her words to the tune of an old Beatles' number. Her version was accompanied by a tambourine and small drum, with not an electric organ or audience in sight.

I took out a coffee and a few toffees and asked her where she got such a song from, and could she tone it down as a crowd just now was the last thing I needed, at which point she interrupted with odd comments, followed by a cackle that any rooster would be proud of.

I began to toy with the idea of silencing the Bag Lady. I could take her inside, I thought, fill her up with toffees and coffee, maybe even a Fisherman's Friend; but then Kay and Sheryl arrived with a bag of chocolate meringues and cream.

They looked annoyingly purposeful. Kay said that they had been talking to Shifty in the Argyll last night and Sheryl even said that Shifty was worried about me. *Worried about me?* I almost walked into the shop and locked the door; I mean, how was that supposed to make me feel good?

"I could care less," I snapped. *If a man takes what he wants with no thought of the aftermath, then worrying about the mess afterwards is just words.*

"You should trust the stars," interrupted the Bag Lady. "I do and look where they have got me."

Kay laughed, "sitting on the concrete, with no memory of a song."

The Bag Lady pressed a chord on her organ and started her song again.

Kay walked into the shop and let the door slam behind her; she was not in the mood for 'nonsense', as she put it. Kay, a woman who never does things by halves, was, according to Sheryl, on a mission to flatten her stomach and was eating nothing but red wine and meat, which is chicken for her as she doesn't touch red meat. According to Sheryl, her new man had said something and Kay was determined to make him eat his words.

"Chicken is the devil's food," the Bag Lady shouted to the slammed door, "and animals that lay eggs should be revered, not eaten."

Kay pulled a face through the window, and then made herself comfortable on the couch beside the half-price basket of books. We watched Kay as she lifted my *Dare to be Nice* book and opened it.

"Her sugar withdrawals are at their peak just now," muttered Sheryl.

My heart bled for her.

Sheryl, as usual, was looking annoyingly content and for the first time ever I didn't really want her around. As I said, Sheryl is looking through the world with lovesick glasses. The world is a grand place when you haven't started fighting over the TV remote yet, when you are happy to sit through their TV programme taking up one seat instead of two. Reason shuts down like an out of date generator and cynicism is tossed aside like a used teabag; all because you are in love and in a constant state of pleasure.

Sheryl is so loved up at the moment she makes Mavis look depressed. She has even warmed to Lumpy and had him and Mavis around for dinner; apparently Lumpy did the pudding. According to Sheryl it was to die for. And Mavis was ecstatic.

"Any man," said Mavis, "who can make a pudding so delicious you don't want to have seconds to spoil the memory is worth a second chance at love, life and happiness."

"She said that?" I looked at Sheryl. "Why would anyone say that?"

"She had knocked back most of the cava at the time," Sheryl laughed. "You know what that does to her."

There is nothing more sickening than happiness when you have none. And right now, with Mavis's cava love, Sheryl's wedded bliss and Kay going carb free for some man in the forestry, I felt nothing but anger. Why did they think coming around to see me in such a state of joy would help?

I wanted them to bugger off and leave me with my lopsided fringe, the Bag Lady and my chocolate. How do you get rid of well-meaning friends without scaring them off for good?

And then, from nowhere, I heard a lone piper warming up with some melancholy tune that would depress even a lottery winner. *Now I have depression piped into the air*. Then the Bag Lady started to shout her song again, over the top of the pipes like some sergeant major school teacher at a sports day.

If the pipes were loud, she was like a foghorn; her high-pitched voice sailed through the street and cut into the pipe music, reminding everyone to come to the book shop, to come and visit me, depressed and fragile. Enough was enough. Anxious not to attract attention and desperate not to have to face people with small talk, I asked the Bag Lady to give up the music and come inside. The Bag Lady instantly stopped, with her hand in mid-air above her drum. She looked shocked (as did Sheryl) and delighted (not like Sheryl); she lifted her mug of coffee with God knows what floating around it, and asked, "And this?"

"Yeah, you can take that as well, but you're not playing any music and you can leave the blanket outside."

Kay was sitting in her usual place on the couch with her feet up on a pile of books waiting to be priced. Sheryl sat next to her, and both were flipping between a coffee table book about male underwear in the '50s and a caveman diet book. I pulled out a chair for the Bag Lady, which she refused; instead she sat on the floor by the Delia cardboard cut-out, stating that a 'stuffed turkey was never truly stuffed until it was carved'; which everyone ignored.

It was Sheryl who suggested (with a look at the Bag Lady) burning a half-priced lavender candle, which had been sitting in the window for well past its sell-by date. And it was Kay who suggested the wine and cheese. "It's all I can eat apart from chicken, which herself here has forbidden," she said.

Sheryl's choice of cheese was impressive; Kay, however, went for a box of rough red and plastic cups. We spent ages talking about music, which the Bag Lady took as an insult, until we persuaded her to tell us more of her stories accompanied by background music of her choice. She chose *Chants and Dances of the Native American Indians*. An impressive choice, I thought.

To be honest it was a choice between that and a collection of pan pipes from the Andes, or Celtic Connection's greatest hits. Our CD shelf had run down due to Rodger and me disputing over what was world music and what Lochgilphead was ready for, and I drew the line totally at Rodger's passion for country and western.

Sheryl was curious about all that had happened in the hospital and asked me to tell all. I was torn, it was painful stuff. And I knew that Kay's ability to be kind depended on how much wine she'd had and, by the looks of how quickly she was knocking it back, she had probably reached her compassion limit, and passed it.

"Exorcise all emotions," said the Bag Lady, "and make room for some healing."

Kay topped up her glass.

Sheryl urged me to talk, and it took at least three glasses and half a tub of Philadelphia to find the courage to tell the tale: the tale of my trip with the man who is the love of my life's new love of his life.

"Does that make sense?" said Kay, gingerly unwrapping runny brie. Sheryl lit another candle.

"On the way to the hospital, he was taking the corners way too fast and overtaking like a moron," I said. "So to distract him I put on some Egyptian drumming."

"That would distract a Buddhist monk in a trance," muttered Kay.

"Shifty went mental and changed it to *Islands in the Stream*, and started singing it!"

"Hate that song," said Kay.

"Oh, I love it," said Sheryl. *Probably one of hers and Steven's, they have so many.*

"By the time Dolly joined in, I had had enough. I pulled it out and slid in a chill-out Arabian style CD. Shifty, who crunches gears like a dog on a bone, then ejected the CD. He said it was doing his head in; I said for him to slow down. And then he asked if I could shut up as he was not a woman and he could not concentrate and listen to bullshit at the same time!"

"No!"

"Really?"

"Yes." I cut off a bit of stilton.

"And then he pulled into McDonald's. He must have felt guilty because he went inside and bought me a bag of nuggets and a filter coffee."

"Their filter is bearable," muttered Kay.

I slapped the stilton on a Jacobs and ate it in two bites, as Sheryl asked about the journey home. "How did that go?" she asked.

"On the way home? Well, I just took all his Dolly Parton CDs out of the car and dumped them in the bin, and he didn't say a word."

"No!"

"Seriously?"

The Bag Lady clapped her hands.

"After which," I said, "I caught the bus home."

However, it wasn't long before curiosity and wine got the better of Kay; she is a straight woman who, after years of fostering children, has learnt to say how it is. In fact she is so good at saying how it is that she not only reformed an alcoholic and then dumped him, but got a job for an agency collecting debts. And according to her new man she loves it.

Her blunt ways have rubbed a lot of people up the wrong way; there is not one shop in Lochgilphead that has not had to face her 'you call this service?' speech. Chubby the butcher refused to serve Kay for a while over some issue about beef sausages and how much beef was actually in them. The arguments ran for months in the comments page of the *Fyne News* and it was one of the few arguments Kay lost. Chubby had, in the end, been true to her word, and Kay was forced to retract her 'scrapings from the floor' accusations and Kay didn't bat an eye.

So when she asked me how I had not seen the obvious in Shifty's gay old ways, I wasn't surprised. Rather, I was dreading it. Sympathy with Kay doesn't come cheap, it comes with uncomfortable questions and possible 'you're an idiot' responses, especially after half a box of wine.

"I thought it was some private joke between the two of you," I said.

Kay snorted. "Yeah right, no straight man would take that as a joke."

"Well, I just thought they were friends and liked building things together."

"Shifty treated the shed like it was his second home, and spent a ridiculous amount of time in there with Rodger. What did you think they were doing, making homebrew?" Kay topped up her glass.

"Well, actually, yes I did."

"Only a fool would not have put the two together."

"But Shifty, he's so macho; I mean, he practically built the shed and he installed special lighting. I remember because Rodger barbequed every decent vegetable in the garden as a thank you, even his giant marrow."

They all started to laugh, even the Bag Lady.

"He was saving that for the Mid Argyll show. He always saves his marrow for the show." I could feel myself welling up. "I just thought they were building, barbequing buddies, mates doing man's stuff."

"She has a point," said Sheryl.

"Macho doesn't mean straight and as for barbequing only an idiot would think that equals straight," said Kay.

"A barbeque does not make a man, neither does a hedge cutter," interrupted the Bag Lady, who had helped herself to a few of Rodger's pens.

Sheryl, trying to shut the Bag Lady up, offered her some cheese. "It's easy to pretend," she muttered. "Love doesn't just die because your man turns out to be something different."

Kay rolled her eyes. "Big words often mean small things," said the Bag Lady, "and the sixth sense is not always as obvious as you would think." Sheryl passed the Bag Lady more cheese, this time on a cracker covered in relish.

"Didn't you ever wonder?" Kay asked.

"Remember," said the Bag Lady, "questions are just unanswered answers, just tell yourself this and you will find out what you need to know."

"Oh, for Christ's sake, shut up!" Kay snapped. She stood up. Apparently she had had enough. She said she couldn't take anymore bullshit quotes, or cheese without crackers, and besides her man would be home soon, looking for a roast with all the low carb trimmings.

Kay left me a pretty empty wine box. "Keep the wine," she shouted, "and remember, keep your chin up, there are plenty more marrows in the garden." She gave me a rough pat on my shoulder. "Things always look better in the morning." She looked at my wine glass. "Well, maybe not tomorrow, but soon." And with an 'I'm still on your side' look she left, which is pretty much all you can expect from Kay.

The Bag Lady lifted the wine box. Not much sloshed about, which is also what you could expect from Kay.

The Bag Lady broke open the wine box, pulled out the bag, cut open the corner and with great concentration dribbled the remains of the wine into my glass. Then she pulled a toffee from under her sleeve, unwrapped it, dropped it in my wine and handed me the glass.

Chapter Seventeen

STILETTO HEELS AND BERYL

A courgette is just a small marrow, but much tastier

The Bag Lady talked about courgettes and watched us drink while she helped herself to the toffees and even ate my meringue, and then, when she saw the school children outside, she left and went back to her spot.

According to Sheryl people were more than talking about the Bag Lady; some were even starting to write into the paper with the occasional complaint about her filthy blanket and more. I had no idea and I didn't even care, she smiled so easily and jigged when excited. How anyone can make a complaint is beyond me; there are worse things a person can do than make up their own words to songs and smell too much.

The Bag Lady, sucking on a Fisherman's Friend, plonked herself onto her blanket and began to call out to the children. She had come up with a story, she said, and now she wanted to tell all to anyone who wanted to listen. Soon she had the high school kids forgetting about their chips, Sheryl coming back for more, and me feeling strangely inspired. She told the story about an old man taking charge, *rising from the ashes of a sheltered home complex that fed, watered and quietened him with pills.*

"He could still tap dance," she said, "sing a song, and the day he did had them all asking for more."

That night I walked home from the shop, thinking about the Bag Lady's ridiculous story that cheered me up so much I felt like eating more than chocolate again. And as I walked past the Ardrishaig car park I saw herself wheeling her bread trolley behind the church and I decided to follow. Anything to put off going home to an empty house and now dark shed. I had been alone before and it is something I never really forgot or wanted to go through again.

The Bag Lady and I sat by the shore, and I watched her pull apart the bread and line up the bits like soldiers beside her. The geese swam up to the shoreline and just like the bits of bread also stood in a line.

I told her that her stories were much better than her singing and then because she didn't answer and because I didn't want to go home, I told her mine.

Years ago when I left my first stiletto-loving ex, I faced loneliness head on. There is nothing to fear but fear itself, some arsehole said, and I believed him and faced my fears in Turkey with a new pair of shoes for company.

Where else would a woman go to learn to be a better belly dancer? I thought massages in the steam baths and sun upon the skin was all a woman would need to feel good again. I pictured myself sitting outside a café like someone in a Jackie Collins novel. I imagined myself walking along the street with my hair flowing like a model in a shampoo commercial, feeling alluring and successful; wishful thinking.

Being single and alone isn't glamorous at all; there is nothing carefree about sitting in a café by yourself, I found it scary. And as for 'the joy of finding yourself', I have yet to find any fulfilment alone. Being alone is being alone, and I hated it; not that I would admit that to anyone, you understand.

Finally, after endless wandering in the heat, I went to a café and tried with a few casual tosses of my hair to look comfortable and when that didn't work; I pulled out a book and read the same lines over and over again.

The coffee didn't last long, one gulp and it was finished, so I moved on to something red, and after half a bottle not only was the moon looking pretty good, but so were half the people sitting about me. The world turns into a friendly place under the influence. Then a fortune-teller came and sat opposite me. "My name is Beryl," she said. And I more than welcomed her and her stained teeth. Candlelight is very forgiving.

Beryl was not so tall; in fact, she was shorter than me and the only time she stopped the traffic was when she didn't read the signs properly. Beryl wasn't much to look at, but she spoke English and was not only prepared to listen to me, she could also attract the attention of a waiter in seconds.

"I have been watching the café," she said, "and you seem alone."

Unimpressed with her obvious observations, I carried on listening. I still had half a bottle to finish and it seemed a lot easier with someone to look at. She lifted my empty cup and peered into the bottom. "I read fortunes; it is my path."

"With an espresso cup?" I said.

"Your future is looking good," she said, continuing to peer. A few grains of coffee dribbled onto the table. "I have a feeling..." she stopped with what seemed the longest pause ever, "in my waters."

I didn't feel anything in my waters, but I humoured her. That is what loneliness abroad does to you, it allows you to humour people you wouldn't be seen dead with back home. After the third bottle was finished (at least I am sure it was the third), she took my hand and read the lines on my palm.

"You have travelled far," she said softly. *Not exactly rocket science.* "But not too far. Britain... Scotland..." *She had been talking to me for about an hour, not hard to work that one out.* "You have much to forgive and even more to remember." *Who hasn't after the age of thirty?* So it went on, and soon I started to feel the warm glow of alcohol-induced empathy. I felt compelled to speak openly about my life, and Beryl was a woman who could listen; there was more to her than a cheap choice of wine and poor dental hygiene.

"Come and see me perform," she finally said. "I am inspirational!"

Beryl was more than inspirational, she was a powerhouse of talk. She had persuaded me to part with the best part of fifty quid for a set of juggling balls. The balls were for me to juggle when stressed; not that I could juggle but as she said when trying to learn to juggle, you can't worry. And I believed her. I took her balls and dog-eared card, and arranged to see her act the next day.

The Fortunes of Tomorrow with Madame B (Beryl to you and me) was held in a quaint boutique hotel claiming to be luxurious.

Beryl had her work cut out for her. The small breakfast room was full of disappointed English people who had been given a free reading from Beryl to compensate for the drainage issues in the bar toilets. And not even the complimentary drinks were warming the audience.

Beryl entered with a swish of black leather, and spoke with a soft elegant voice which, for a moment, held their attention. She was now tall (thanks to really high-heeled boots), blonde (thanks to a pretty good wig), and wore a low-cut top, which, thanks to an excellent corset, pushed up the impossible.

I was looking at a middle-aged grandmother transformed, and poured into leather tight enough to make breathing hard work. And with each trancelike breath, Beryl's chest heaved that bit more, making the men sitting in the front row happy to toss their coins into her pot.

Beryl stood for a moment, like she was in another world and then, pre-empting boredom from the children, she began.

"I am getting something from a gentleman over there... Clues, yes, yes, symbols of nature," she paused, "and the number five is hitting me."

"Like a sledge, honey," shouted a sunburnt woman from the back. Beryl threw her a look that was hard to decipher? Was it a glare or a dare?

She moved closer as her leather-covered thighs swished with each step, her eyes never leaving Mrs Sunburnt. "Are you choosing beauty or strife in your life?" she said.

There was no answer.

Beryl moved away with her back to Mrs Sunburnt and let a loud scream followed by an even louder, "Don't!"

Mrs Sunburnt jumped, we all jumped; then, with great drama, Beryl turned and pointed her leather-clad finger at Mrs Sunburnt and her husband. "I said, don't be distracted by doubt or negativity around you."

Silence. We all waited... what was next?

Beryl looked to the ceiling and then about, like she was hearing voices. "I hear singing, a child's," she paused. "No, no." She looked at her audience. "It's a woman's voice."

"My mother is no singer," muttered Mr Sunburnt.

"It's not your mother," snapped Beryl. "It's a woman calling."

"My mother would be up there cleaning, not singing," continued Mr Sunburnt. A chuckle broke out in the back row.

"I said, it is not your mother."

"My mother's right here," said the young boy on the edge of the Sunburnt clan's row.

Beryl was not put off. With a slow intake of breath inflating her cleavage to Dolly Parton's size, she began to make her way towards the Sunburnt clan. In a low hypnotic voice, she talked about an apple tree, leather straps and a horse called Bubble and Squeak. Soon the whole row was beginning to fill up.

"She loved a good ride," said Granny Sunburnt tearfully.

"I was her favourite," muttered Mr Sunburnt.

"Me too," wept the same young boy and hugged what looked like a very pale sister beside him.

"Symbols," Beryl continued. "I am thinking of a shoe, single, and..." she looked at me, "no socks!"

Beryl was good, a real pro. She had something to say to everyone; she even spoke to me about an Egyptian past. She performed, chanted, and sang for two hours.

"Good comes from a bad situation," she motioned to the blonde in front of me. "There is a time for change."

The blonde's pal interrupted, "We've been telling her that for years. Her man is a no good, two-faced prick."

Beryl jumped in. "As I said, there is a time for change."

"He's been leading her up the garden path" the pal stood up; she was on her fourth can of red bull, and nothing was going to stop her, "for years!"

Beryl, who was by now standing right next to her opposition, placed a hand on Ms Red Bull's shoulder, pushed her down, and shouted, "And a time to cut yourself off from the past; things that may harm you."

"Hear, hear!" shouted the Sunburnt crew.

Beryl grabbed Ms Red Bull's hands. "There is, out there, a lover for you, who will know what you want when you want it." She grabbed the blonde's hands, along with the Ms Red Bull's hand and told them both not to worry about what others think or say, but to be the women you were both meant to be.

Beryl spoke to the women about treasuring their dreams. She berated men for not crying and being true to their feelings until the men began to blubber like babies.

In the end, they all caved in, including the Sunburnt clan.

Beryl had them eating out of her hand like a cat on catnip. A round, ordinary grandma had managed to turn an audience of disgruntled, hungover, sunburnt disbelievers into a crowd of weeping converts, happily tossing coins into Beryl's bucket like breadcrumbs to the ducks. Beryl had worked the audience as easily as a prostitute with servicemen on leave and had, in the end, walked away with a pot full of lira AND the odd euro thrown in.

I watched, learned and absorbed every trick. Beryl had nothing more going for her than a decent chest and a lot of balls. If she could do it, so could I. If she could hold an audience, why couldn't I? Inspired, I decided never to be a student again. I was going to take my chest, my hips and all that I learned from Beryl back to Britain and find a way, like Beryl, to have an audience eating out of my hand.

I looked at the Bag Lady staring at the waves on a rock. A fat lot of good following that experience did me. Inspired by Beryl, I won and lost at belly dancing, won and lost at love yet again, and was now seriously thinking of befriending a bag lady because I couldn't bear the thought of an empty house.

"Loneliness is a complete bastard," I said to the Bag Lady.

"Aye, but Beryl gave you a good story to tell."

I handed her half of my Mars bar. It was gone so quick I handed her the other half.

"The geese are fed, but I have not seen the swans today," she said.

I wondered if she did really sleep in the graveyard or if she slept at all, then without even thinking about it I asked if she wanted to come back for more Mars bars. To be honest, I couldn't bear the thought of being alone in a house so empty that even a blaring TV couldn't fill it.

And, besides, my instincts to an extent had worked before in Turkey.

Chapter Eighteen

THE TEE PEE

Splitting up is as easy as splitting hairs

When I asked the Bag Lady back for a chocolate she jumped at the chance. She disappeared to the back of the church to collect her things, oblivious of anyone staring at her. I watched her slim erect figure say goodnight to the geese, while she packed up her belongings in a backpack. She wasn't a pretty sight and even worse when she laughed, which she frequently did at the geese.

I knew Sheryl and Kay would say I was mad. And I guess I was really, who knows what she might do. Kay (ever the optimist) says she's on something, but as I said to Kay, "What would she be on, and how would she get it? A GP? Some dodgy deal behind the shop with a free song?"

"No," I said to Kay. "The Bag Lady is not on anything. She's a one off." She is a mystery with a past that she can't even remember, or maybe she doesn't even want to.

But to me, she was the light in my black hole of a life and, from the looks of it, Puss's as well. She had given me a reason to get up in the morning, even if it was just to find out what insane thing she was going to say that day.

The Bag Lady followed me home; she trotted beside me carrying her possessions while humming some unrecognisable tune.

I asked her what her name was, and she said that she had many, most of which she chose to forget.

"But what were you born with?" I said.

"What you are born with is not what you die with, and I am interested in neither," she said, and I stopped asking after that.

That night she built a campfire and made herself at home on the shed veranda. I brought her out some hot chocolate with cream, a blanket I knew I no longer wanted, and emptied the kitchen of anything remotely chocolaty. She polished off the chocolate-covered raisins and the yogurt-covered raisins and then, with a mouthful of fruit and nut, she looked at me across the burning embers of the campfire.

"Past lives are past," she said, "you are who you are," which is exactly what Beryl told me years ago.

Once we arrived at my home I offered the Bag Lady the shed, but she refused, even when I explained that it had plumbing.

"Water," she said, "should come from outside, not from within." *Except for tea, coffee and whatever else I gave her in the shop, but what's the point of splitting hairs with a mad woman?*

"I like the wind at my heels and the midges in my hair," she said. "I like the smell of damp and the feel of wet mud between my toes," she cackled, and rubbed her toes into the grass.

By the time I had gone into the house and come back out with two glasses of Rodger's finest elderflower bubbly, she had erected her tee pee and built a campfire, and I didn't even bat an eyelid. Instead I rolled over a round bit of wood from the log pile to sit on and joined in. *Welcome to the mad world of the Goose Lady*, I thought, and Rodger's elderflower had never tasted so good.

We spent the night watching the fire, with Puss sleeping like a sphinx beside it and, in the end, I didn't notice the Bag Lady's aroma, even though the midges did; I wasn't bitten once that night.

The next morning I woke to the Bag Lady playing on her organ and singing.

I looked out my bedroom window and there she was outside, sitting cross-legged on her blanket next to a small fire, with her black greasy hair hanging down her back.

She gave me a wave.

I headed down to find that Puss had beaten me. She was sitting by the fire with that dozy expression cats usually have when basking in the sun. And Puss, along with the Bag Lady, looked happy. I was taken aback. Who's happy in the morning? I don't know anyone who is happy in the morning, even loved-up Mavis and Sheryl look two espressos short of a smile in the morning.

And from what I can see the Bag Lady has nothing to be happy about. She smells so bad that you have to sit downwind to breathe and she carries everything she owns on her back. She even sleeps on the ground, in Scotland, with no mattress.

I was drawn to her like a kid to a Christmas tree.

Sheryl told me I was not only mad, but a complete idiot. She said people laughed at the Bag Lady.

"There is not enough homebrew in the world that would make breathing in a small space with her bearable," Sheryl said.

"She does take a bit of getting used to," I muttered.

Kay's words were more pointed. "You are *off your trolley*; getting used to her is not something sane people do. On a good day, you feel sorry for her and on a bad day you ignore her. Either way you toss her a coin and walk on. You don't take her home..."

But then they are loved up with little need for comfort, let alone revenge, and like most people, they had something to go home to other than a cat and a bookshop full of shed posters.

The Bag Lady told me stories over her campfire. It was the end of summer and the nights were long and warm. By the time the sun was down, the Bag Lady's fire was often a mere smoulder and Puss had made herself at home in the tee pee. I never ventured into the tee pee, looking inside was bad enough.

Every morning I woke to her calling me with her song and the tea on the fire. I would go down in my slippers and dressing gown, which was beginning to smell like a kipper, pull up the same log and sip her tea; it was the worse stewed tea ever, but it did demolish a hangover quicker than the geese did the WRI egg rolls.

She was always sitting on her blanket cross-legged with bare feet and we both sipped from Rodger's china tea set, the one that he brought back from his antique store. I told her she could use it as long as she liked and she wiggled her toes with glee. She had the most amazing feet, small, perfect and through the grime I could see beautifully formed nails. She can't have been as old as I first thought; no one had feet like that after menopause.

After tea at the same time each morning she would, with no explanation, stand up and leave, and I had no idea where she went until she arrived at *The Read and be Thankful* later. And then she would disappear again and return later in the evening. I could tell when she arrived because Puss would disappear. I would hear the cat flap shut, then from out of the patio windows I would see the glow of the fire with Puss, who was now completely in love, sitting beside it.

Whenever Puss came into the house she filled the room with a wood fire smell and she never meowed for food anymore, or for that matter appeared to clean herself. It was like Puss had transformed into the Bag Lady's alter ego, and she hadn't even been here a week.

Once Sheryl and I drove past the church and saw the Bag Lady wandering back from the church throwing bread to the geese and swans, with a pile of kids tormenting her and singing.

I did my best to scare them off, reminding them how horrible they were being to a nice elderly woman. I felt better, needed, wanted and quite brave. Although the Bag Lady never thanked me, she stopped in mid toss of breadcrumbs and yelled, "Come away in, there is plenty of bread for all to feed."

One time while the Bag Lady was singing outside the bookshop, Kay and Sheryl explored the back of the church and came across a small buckled coal bunker with nothing but a pile of out-of-date Warburton's loaves and some extra-long matchsticks in it.

"Who has matchsticks these days?" said Kay. I had no idea, but I imagined the Bag Lady wouldn't need a match to start a fire; she looked the type who could rub two sticks together and get a hog roast going.

Kay and Sheryl laughed. They were warming to her, I could tell, especially when Kay came around with a few old blankets for her and a box of fire lighters, for when the rain kicked in again.

At the end of the week over our morning stewed tea, which took half a dozen sugars to drink, the Bag Lady pulled out a scrapbook from her bag and handed it to me.

"Beryl belongs here," she said and then tossed her tea leaves onto the fire along with some dirt, stood up, called Puss to attention, shut the flap on her tent, and was off before Puss even had a chance to lick the butter off the toast she gave her.

To where, I have no idea.

The scrapbook was thick and full of cut-outs of stories from a magazine column and, as I opened the scrapbook, notes and photos fell out. I looked at one of the photographs. Deidre McConical was a young red-haired woman who reminded me of a '70s version of Lucille Ball.

Chapter Nineteen

DOMESTIC BLISS

Domestic bliss is complex but achievable

It was the day of Rodger's birthday, the day he got the all clear to come home and his new boyfriend was going to collect him. In three weeks my life had changed from making coffee for a partner who refused to speak, and wondering why, to knowing why and wishing I didn't.

Heading out was the last thing I wanted to do. I wanted to close the shop, go home and hide by the Bag Lady's fire, maybe read a story from her scrapbook. But I needed the keys to the community centre store cupboard. Which meant visiting Lumpy's flat and witnessing the domestic bliss of him and Mavis, which was also the last thing I wanted to do.

I had just received a note and was in a mood that even one of Rodger's homemade brews wouldn't cure. I plonked myself on the white couch, and there it was, a snippy note hanging limply from the mail slot like a stuck toothpick. A note from one of Imogen's latest recruits, who also happened to be a member of the subcommittee of the council for the community centre's steering group.

I mean how long does a title need to be for Pete sake?

The note talked about the importance of moving on. Apparently the adult education department was doing that, but they required prime space, said prime space being the area I used for my equipment. It was no longer needed as my classes were empty, so I had been told to move my things as soon as possible.

Apparently the demand for assertiveness training had taken off like a rocket by the elderly who had signed up and now begun protesting outside the Social about their fifteen minute visits.

Shifty; bloody Shifty.

After a few messages on my phone asking me to 'clear out my equipment' followed by a few more messages stating that my equipment would be skipped if not collected; 'pronto', I was finally sent a note; *your belly dancing gear will, as of tomorrow, be in the hands of the Ardrishaig players* - the Ardrishaig Players were doing Aladdin for their panto this year.

I had to face the music.

I headed for Lumpy's flat. Mavis or Mav and I had sort of made a nodding truce. She had heard about the shed and the birthday boys and according to Sheryl and Kay she felt sorry for me. I guess that's what a robust sex life does to a woman, makes them amicable.

The last time I saw Mav, she was in the post office dealing with a couple from Germany who were looking for a bus to anywhere away from Lochgilphead, and she didn't shout once. Instead she phoned a friend of a friend from the Russian literary class who told her that Russian and German were as similar as whisky and smoothies, but she did have a bus timetable.

Lumpy's was across the road from the centre, and the smell of warm bread wafted across the front yard as I walked up to the gate. It was Mavis who answered the door. She took me into the kitchen where Lumpy was preparing something delicious, and as he didn't want his sauce to spoil, I was forced to stand, watch and wait.

Lumpy was whisking heavily like a pro on the food channel, with his new 'in touch with my feminine side' apron on. Gingham was a new look for Lumpy, inspired by the overdose of Doris Day films they had taken to watching together, so Kay said.

Mavis sat at the table in the kitchen, purring the odd comment to Lumpy: "Easy on the butter, darling"; "Is there any of that lovely cheese left, delicious one?" and "Don't use that cheap whisky in the sauce, precious?" etc. Lumpy and Mavis were definitely an item now and at least half of Lochgilphead had noticed.

It wasn't just the matching purple and the 'darlings' that gave it away. Now they spent most of their time together arm in arm absorbed in each other's company, and having long discussions in the shop about the best sausages. Lumpy and Mavis, it seemed, were living in domestic bliss.

Mavis offered me a coffee and a seat, she asked me if I was a froth or latte person and if I was sure about the whole Bag Lady thing. I did think about replying along the lines of 'are you sure about the whole Lumpy thing and since when did you make froth for your coffee?' but decided to say nothing.

Having Mavis talking to me was much more preferable.

I watched Lumpy in his apron and nylon tracksuit bottoms and wondered if he ever cared about what he looked like.

"Women, we're always obsessed about our looks," I said. "But men, the ones I have known, don't seem to care at all."

"What has a face got to do with anything?" said Lumpy, a profound statement from someone whose face was nothing to write home about. Although now, since the great union, it is looking softer and less granite-like. "I mean, look at me and herself, it's not about the face for us, is it, Mav?"

Mavis sat up. "What do you mean? I've just had my eyebrows done. Are you telling me that it was a waste of time?"

"I didn't say that, honey," said Lumpy. "I meant..." He looked down at his pan, with an 'oh bollocks, my sauce has gone over' comment.

"I spend a lot of time on my face," she said. "Don't you like looking at it?"

Lumpy didn't answer; he was absorbed in his sauce crisis.

"Are you saying I'm ugly?"

Lumpy was stirring like mad and getting nowhere.

Mavis looked at me and then back at the 'delicious one'. "Lumpy, don't you like the way I look?"

Lumpy looked up. "No, I mean yes." He looked at me. "I mean, no, sorry, yes?" He smeared his hands across his gingham front and looked at his other half. "Cupcake, I never said you were ugly, it's just that there is more to you than that and that is what I like about you."

Mavis was wearing her new purple leisure suit and looked nothing like a cupcake and more like a tea cosy. Lumpy dumped his sauce and pointed to the keys hanging on the door, as Mavis demanded to know exactly what that was.

"You know what I mean," he said, scrubbing his pan clean for the next batch. "You are just you, the way you are, all cuddly and warm and... and complex."

I decided to leave soon after that. I took the key and made a discreet exit as they began to argue about how to save a cheese sauce, does cuddly mean fat and the need for eyebrow waxing. Not once did they mention the Gala day, although Lumpy did at one point offer to collect my things once he redid his sauce, but Mav wasn't having any of it. She gave me a 'this is private' look and I, ever the sensitive type, took the hint.

Domestic bliss, it seems, is a tough boat to row.

I made for the door wondering if perhaps I should look into adult education when I overheard Mav say to Shifty, "She hasn't a clue about the gathering tomorrow, poor cow."

Poor cow, indeed. I knew all about Rodger and Shifty's get together, 'we're a couple' celebration in the Argyll. And I also knew all about the surprise birthday cake made by Imogen. Who, according to Mavis, bakes low fat goodies to die for, probably in Lycra and with some sort of jumping jack music in the background.

I knew all about it because Betty had taken a liking to the Bag Lady, and she had been visiting. And I also knew that I could, if I wanted to, take advantage of the new friendship.

Chapter Twenty

THE HOMECOMING

Goatees are for goats, and any man who thinks otherwise is just kidding himself.

When Rodger was discharged from hospital he moved into the Argyll. He was wheeled into the public bar like a wounded Vietnam War veteran and greeted with mixed messages of welcome and disapproval from Betty, Shifty's mother. Betty had no idea about the liaison until the van incident, and she was in shock. She thought that Shifty was still trying to woo his ex back.

"All that tofu and yoga," she said. "I thought it was for her, not him"; *Shifty had, for a while explored vegetarianism.* "Who would have known it? My Duncan would be spinning in his urn if he knew."

Shifty promised his mother that Rodger would help. The Argyll struggled like all hotels in a small town, and "having a resident artist like Rodger," said Shifty, "may help." Besides, he had plans, big plans, and the means to follow them through.

Betty was not completely convinced. In the past Shifty was known to say anything to get his way. When Duncan died, Shifty convinced his mother to hand over the hotel. "He promised me the earth, and all I got was a new bedroom," she said, ignoring the fact that the hotel now made a profit rather than a loss.

Shifty and Rodger had their work cut out for them.

Betty was the sort of woman who considered palm reading scientific, who religiously read her star sign every day and made decisions by it. And when Shifty took over the first thing to go was Betty's decision-making process. "Star signs," he said, "do not understand recessions."

"That's not what your father said."

"Well, he is not here. I am, and I will make this place work, not some Zodiac bullshit."

But Betty was a woman with her own mind. She had planned to have the Argyll spiritually cleaned after her Duncan died because she wanted a meeting with her dead husband.

"Work in the hotel was empty without him," she said, "and there are memories of him everywhere. The corners where he had his cigarettes, the book room where he had his stash of adult 'literature' and the kitchen now quiet."

"That's because they are working, Mother."

"The hotel is like a foreign country to me," Betty complained.

Betty said that the kitchen used to be her favourite room; apparently it was where they had their best arguments. She even took a ladle to him once, according to Shifty; vanilla custard was never the same after that.

"I want a resolution," she said.

Betty was sitting in the bar at the time with the rest of the belly dance class. It was a Monday night and Shifty was pouring tonic and half-price vodkas. Betty had, since her husband died, developed a passion for tonic and whatever on a Monday night with the girls, which at the time was my class of three and Lumpy.

"I want closure," she said.

"So do we all," snapped Kay.

In desperation, Shifty took his mother to the Zumba open day and Imogen's pink Lycra got to her. She forgot all her dreams of having it out with Duncan and spent her time learning Zumba and buying Lycra. She was even one of the students on the now burnt Gala day poster, although her jumping jack was more of a small kick.

When Rodger came home, he and Shifty threw themselves into their new life with not much thought of others. But then people in love always do. They are like people who give up smoking or carbs, they just can't wait to spread the good news. Good news that no one else wants to hear, unless they too are in love.

Shifty, much to his mother's disappointment, had gone all alternative, with blond stubble and new jeans that swung low. I know, because I saw him in the chemist stocking up on E45 cream while his mother was moaning at him to pull up his pants.

Kay says that Rodger made some stupid remark about liking a bit of rough and then the next thing you know Shifty has tossed out the razors and was growing the sort of beard that Betty called a waste of time. Then Rodger made some joke about a bit of rough being a bit rough on his face, and Shifty started bulk-buying E45 cream in the chemist.

Rodger, according to Sheryl via Steven, spent his first few days in the Argyll public bar sitting in a Red Cross wheelchair like a disabled Vincent Van Gogh, occasionally mumbling about vermillion and good lighting. And Betty was unimpressed, but to be fair she wasn't particularly impressed with Shifty's ex either.

Not that I'm jealous or anything; but sitting by the Bag Lady's fire at night and hearing Betty who'd taken to visiting every day, talk about the couple as she did, did give me some pleasure., especially when it involved feeding her Rodger's now dwindling homebrew.

Rodger appeared a few weeks later on the second page of the *Fyne News* with his newly sprouted beard, I was unmoved.

There he was, with a brush in his hand, and Shifty holding up his latest artistic work like he had done it. And there was even a full page article about him, the brave artist *toeing the line;* like he was some sort of hero...

Lochgilphead artist, Rodger, nearly said goodbye to months of commissioned work, thanks to a collision with a van and reconstructive surgery (it was a toe!). *Rodger, however, is determined, and carries on regardless.*

The article continued along the 'great artist' theme, mentioning Rodger's previous works including the Flower of Scotland exhibition, and finished with:

Shifty has even hung one of Rodger's pieces in the Argyll, and invites anyone to view and write comments!

There was also another photo of Rodger's painting of his feet for the whole of Argyll to see. Rodger's feet are the least attractive thing about him; they are positively ugly, and having such feet reproduced in pastels, even in abstract form, didn't do them any favours. I always warned Rodger against the wisdom of sandals but he never listened.

The locals, according to Kay, are unmoved by Rodger's abstract drawing; in fact, they are so uninterested they haven't even asked what the painting in the bar is supposed to be. Betty even hung a coat over it once. Of course the painting is not to Betty's taste. Neither is Shifty carrying Rodger up the stairs like something out of *Gone with the Wind*, as she liked to put it. But then Betty does like to exaggerate even more than Mavis.

But despite the setbacks Kay says that they seemed blissfully happy, not that I wanted to listen. It's not easy hearing that your ex has moved on, when your own world revolves around getting over the split. There are constant reminders everywhere, which is the big disadvantage of living in a small town; whatever you do is always noted and talked about. Handy if you want a good attendance at a funeral, but not so handy if you have done something stupid, or, as in my case, would like to forget what you have lost.

There is only one street in Lochgilphead that matters and leads to anything of note, the Main Street and it was difficult for me to avoid the happy couple. I would be walking down that one main street, thinking about the latest self-help book I was reading or which chocolate bar I should now try, and then like from nowhere, just as I was popping out of the newsagents, I would see Shifty and Rodger, laughing. Or I would bump into Shifty and Rodger out of the chemist, smiling, or walk past them sitting in the Stables having a coffee by the window, talking. The worst was seeing them standing outside the shop talking with whoever was collecting for whatever charity which, thanks to the absence of the Bag Lady outside the Co-op, had started again.

Sometimes they noticed me and said hello, other times they were so engrossed in each other they didn't and to be honest I didn't know which was worse.

Then by far the mother of all days was when Imogen was handing out posters. Apparently the Bag Lady had cheesed her off so much that Imogen now felt that her feeding the geese in Ardrishaig was a threat to the safety of the community and she was making a point. The fact that she was walking the main street with the Bag Lady singing in the background from the bookshop seemed to me quite ironic.

I had heard about it, but had not taken any of it in. After all, Betty had told me and as I said she was prone to exaggerate. Especially since she, along with Mavis, had revolted from the Zumba class. It started with the YouTube video, from the Gala day when only Betty's right foot could be seen, and then it escalated after the line-up for the Argyll 'Prance and Pose' day was announced and neither were in it. The Argyll didn't have room for all of the class so only a select few were asked. Mavis didn't cut it.

I was walking past the chemist and saw the first of many posters. I felt angry, especially when I saw Imogen strutting down the other side of the street with a handful of posters hanging out of her leather satchel.

Imogen looked long, lean and annoyingly eye-catching with a matching leather jacket and long flickable blonde hair. If I was honest, I would say she belonged in a Californian shampoo or 'Botox really works' advertisement. But I am not. I am bitter, and she looked out of place in Lochgilphead and completely up herself, making me regret my lack of waxing. She saw me and waved and I waved back.

I watched her go into the butcher's shop, laughing as Chubby began to flirt. Not an easy accomplishment for a butcher in a white coat tainted with blood, and a short haircut. But I have to say Chubby pulled it off; taking the act of sharpening a knife to new heights of sensuality I had never seen before...not counting Rodger's Highland fling in the good old days, that is.

But when I saw Chubby post the poster on the butcher's door along with the funeral notices I felt sick to my stomach. Only real posters landed there, and for the first time I seriously worried about the Bag Lady's future.

Chapter Twenty-One

CUSTODY

Revenge is never sweet, only the beginning of something worse.

A few days after the centre page spread Shifty contacted me about the shed. Since Rodger's stay in the hospital, the shed remained unused and forgotten (*like me*), and Rodger was missing it (*not like me*). Rodger wanted the shed with him, at the back of the Argyll, so presumably he could go from the adoration in the pub to the artistic solitude in the shed.

I told Shifty via Kay that I liked the shed where it was and to tell Rodger that, as it was he who moved and ruined my pyramid for his damn shed, he could get stuffed.

"The shed is part of the garden," I said, "and the sooner I can persuade the Bag Lady to move in, the better."

Kay looked at me with a mixture of disappointment and pity. She knew the chances of the Bag Lady moving into the shed were as probable as her never playing *Come on Eileen* again. She called me petty, and told me I was behaving like a spoilt cow.

"In the end it is only you that you are hurting," she said, sounding like every other know-it-all on the planet. And then she went on to tell me how passionate Rodger was about the shed, *like I didn't know that,* and how it was where he and Shifty met and where he discovered his new direction.

"You can't deny him that!" she said. "Have you no dignity?"

She's been drinking with the enemy, I knew it! "Fuck dignity," I said.

"Kinda expected that from you, but parting should be amicable."

"Like you and your ex?"

"He was an alcoholic," said Kay. "He was never sober."

"If Rodger wants his shed, he can shove it up his plaster cast," I snapped. "Tell him to come and get it himself; see how far he gets with that in a wheelchair!"

Kay was not impressed; she was standing in the bookshop with Sheryl, and Sheryl was now caught between the two of us; pointing out that Rodger was no longer in a wheelchair.

Sheryl and I had been in the process of demolishing a whipped cream special while Sheryl was trying to tell me how important it was to move on, and think about the positive changes I could make in my life.

"Like the shop, and Rodger's shed posters," I said, thinking of what destruction I could do to them. Sheryl, like Kay, looked unimpressed.

"Splitting up is splitting up, you have to work out who gets what first," she said. It seemed Sheryl was beginning to choose sides.

Kay had taken the stance of a foster parent or head teacher from hell and she was determined to administer a lecture on behaviour and disappointment, about being realistic and acting like an adult. A lecture that I had heard before and probably will hear again; the sort of lecture that would make a conformist rebellious, and made me feel like a fifteen-year-old caught coming home late, half cut.

Kay then moved onto her favourite subject, decluttering and how it worked miracles. "You should clear the decks and then start afresh, it's good for the soul."

I told her that the 'new me' had no time to listen and wanted to kick the arse into the past of anyone who said different. Then I asked what should I do first, work out who gets what or declutter.

Ignoring me completely, Kay continued. "When my ex left," she said, "I spent a week filling up a skip and not only lost a stone, but learnt to laugh again!"

Personally I find the idea of Kay laughing hard to believe.

Kay looked at the message machine bleeping by the cash register;

she had been itching to play it back all afternoon, and asked me why I hadn't. We all knew what was on it, Shifty, on Rodger's behalf, asking me to be reasonable, and as I said to Sheryl, "Who is reasonable when their heart is broken through no fault of their own?" Kay naturally disagreed with me.

"No fault of your own? Putting up with you is only possible on a part time basis and with a decent amount of booze."

"Cheers, Kay!"

"And what are you going to do when he gives up asking?" she added. "He has rights, you know, he is entitled to half of everything."

"Then he can cut the bloody thing in half," I said.

"Don't be childish. How will it stand up if it is in half?"

"That's for the DIY specialist to work out, not me," I said.

"So this is what you want?" said Kay, with her typical hands on hips stance. "War?"

Sheryl told Kay to take it easy. "It's early days," she said. "Can't you remember what that was like?"

Actually, if I was truthful, up till now I had no idea what I wanted. It was like the fight had gone out of me, and there was nothing left. Every morning as I woke to the sight of Rodger's chandelier, I knew that I should do something. But what? Just now making coffee took all my energy, that and working out what change to give each customer. In fact, if it hadn't been for the Bag Lady, I probably would not have even opened the shop. I had at times felt okay in a sort of 'I don't want to get out of bed, but I'd better' way; until Rodger started leaving notes under my front door and Shifty started leaving messages on my machine demanding the shed.

For some reason I saw rage and wanted blood, tears and anguish, but not mine. Rodger had knocked me down and now I wanted to kick his feet from under him. I started to dream about getting even. I imagined the Bag Lady taking over the shed, filling it with her stained electric organ, her dusty drum, her smelly blanket and of course her brown bag full of rolled up tissues and socks, stinking it out big time.

I even fantasized about burning the shed, running outside like a wild witch performing some sort of ritual involving petrol, chanting and bare feet... *Revenge is sweet, revenge is mine and I'm taking it with both hands!*

I wanted to inflict as much pain on Rodger and Shifty as they had inflicted on me. I wanted my pint of tears... his tears, I wanted to march into the Argyll and balance on Rodger's sore leg until he cried, like I had cried for nights, but, as Sheryl pointed out, if he was crying it would hardly be on my shoulder.

"I am not giving up the shed," I muttered. "Herself out there uses it for her washing."

Kay looked at me like I was reading a joke from a Christmas cracker and expected a laugh. "Once, just once, the Bag Lady hung her socks in the veranda and they weren't even wet."

Kate was beating me, verbally berating me like Maggie Thatcher in the Commons. I told her that she wasn't much of a friend and asked whose side was she on. Kay said nothing.

"Nice never got me anywhere," I finally muttered, Sheryl looked at me like she knew what I was talking about.

Kay asked me when was I ever nice, and I gave her best, 'feel sorry for Neff' ever story...I told her about my ex and the stiletto wearer. I told her how after the split, he had arranged for us to meet in some grimy pub, miles from Norwich. A pub where I was forced to listen to him list the reasons why living with me wasn't easy.

"At least the stiletto wearer had the decency to sit in the corner and pretend to be a punter," I said. "But I could tell those shoes anywhere. Women's shoes are like fingerprints to a shoe-loving woman."

"Mavis told me," said Sheryl quietly.

"I told him I wanted half the value of the café and the stiletto wearer, who obviously was listening, turned on me from across the room, while she was on her mobile! 'Look, lush of the year', she shouted, like something out of a Dick Tracy novel, 'you're not getting anything but a free exit out of here'."

"Dick Tracy, huh?" said Kay.

"There was me sitting in some dive of a pub with some young thing in a skirt that barely covered the essentials. A woman who looked as rough as the cement on my drive was trying to make me squirm, intimidate me. Well, it worked. I've got nothing of the ex; all those years of cleaning tables for what? A five-year-old moped and matching leathers?"

"Maybe there was nothing to give," said Sheryl. "Maybe it was all gone? Look at Kay. Her ex lost everything. She had to start again, with a man on a forestry wage."

"Cheers, Sheryl."

I looked outside the shop window. The Bag Lady had a small audience of school children as she told another story. A story for teenagers, about revenge "getting even," she said, "is never the end, but always the beginning of something worse". I wondered if she had been listening to us in the shop, or even worse, reading my thoughts.

"Why do I have to suffer?" I said to the girls. "I didn't ask for any of this. All I seem to do is lose and losing is not easy. In fact, nothing prepares you for loss," I muttered. "Nothing. Even if you have felt loss before, it still hits you like new. Every time it happens, the loss of a dream, of hope, of everything you've worked for... the pain is fresh like you never felt it before."

Sheryl and Kay looked at me with pity. *The worst thing ever...*

"You could always get a clothes line," Kay finally said.

"Or fix the pyramid," said Sheryl. "I'll help."

They just didn't get it, did they? "It's not about the socks," I said. "The shed is where we hang out, Betty, me and sometimes even Iona."

I looked outside the window; the Bag Lady had finished her story and told the boys she had food to eat.

"Enough is enough," she said and started to tuck into her chips and cheese panini when Betty arrived on the scene. Betty handed her a packet of crisps and a carton of, I suspect, the Argyll's soup of the day. Betty said that taking food from the hotel to the Bag Lady was the highlight of the day; she knew it riled her son. And for the first time the Bag Lady turned down the soup.

The Bag Lady lived on chips and sauce during the week, as well as whatever I gave her with coffee, and at the weekends her pickings were much more refined as the mothers of those children visited with snacks. Today had been a day of both teenagers and mothers.

Kay pressed the message machine on.

"Neff, I want to talk to you about the shed. Can you phone or come into the pub?"

"Neff, I know this is difficult for you, but we need to sort out the shed."

"Neff, you know full well that the shed is Rodger's, and I know full well you're not too busy to answer."

Well, I am busy. Busy, busy, busy with your shed posters and your clothes in the wardrobe and feeding your cat.

"Fuck's sake, pick up the phone!"

"Why are you putting up a fight about the shed? I know you, what you going to use it for?"

"The documents are in the post. You have a month to clear out, so don't fill it with your belly dancing bullshit!"

Kay pressed pause. "How many messages are there? Can you not just put the guy out of his misery? Why do you have to be so difficult?"

"Difficult?" I said, "why not; if Rodger can have a 'new Rodger', I can have a new difficult me."

I was about to say more when we heard a cackle from the front.

This time it was Betty's cackle; the Bag Lady was telling her one of my favourite *elderly men makes a break for freedom* stories, and Betty was loving it.

"I am all ears!!!" she said.

The Bag Lady had set the scene like a pro she always did for Betty, and today she had excelled herself. Even I wanted to listen and I had heard it all before but each time the Bag Lady told it just that little bit better.

"Let me tell you a story," she said, "with a beginning a middle and no end; of how five men of the age where taking Viagra would be suicidal, take up stripping and get caught."

Betty was ecstatic, "I'm ready."

I stared out of the shop window into the dark street. The shop was empty and I was on my own. Kay and Sheryl had gone home and the Bag Lady had left to go wherever she always went to at the end of the day, I suspect to feed the geese and swans. I wondered about whether they really could move her on, and, if so, where, and what would I do.

The only time I felt like myself was when I was sitting by the campfire drinking her stinking tea. When I was with her, I forgot all my pain.

I switched on the message machine again.

"Pick up the phone!"

"It's just a shed to you."

I switched the message machine off, unplugged it and tossed it in the bin.

Then I saw her strut down the street, Imogen with her leather satchel; she stopped at the Hydro and pulled out a poster.

Chapter Twenty-Two

THE EXHIBITIONISTS

Wake up and smell the crap; it is only then that you can wipe it from your feet.

Rodger was working on a collection of paintings called the 'Frontal Winds of Argyll' when the accident happened. He was collaborating with Martin, Imogen's other half, and owner of the post office along with the *Wee Bit of Art* shop in Oban. Together they were organising an exhibition, as Shifty, according to Martin, was a stabilising influence on Rodger; *as opposed to me, nutcase Neff.*

It was Mavis who told me the next day when I was in the post office returning unwanted purple his and her mugs. *Shifty, apparently, is more a black and white man.*

Mavis told me about the exhibition because, as she stated, she was concerned and her concern was blurted out for everyone to hear. I told her I was grateful for her bluntness, but wondered if it was necessary for everyone in the queue to hear. Truth was, I wondered about Mavis and her motives.

Mavis had fallen in and out of love with Imogen quickly; three months of lessons and one performance to be precise. Now she, along with Betty, wanted revenge. Imogen had promised so much and more. "My stars," she called them. "My little glamour ladies. You shall stand at the front for the video, and shine for us all." Once they saw that 'shining for us all' in the video was just half Mavis's right foot and

Betty's left hand and the rest was hidden behind Imogen, they were up for rebellion. Especially when they had been excluded from the Prance and Pose night in the Argyll.

Betty and Mavis had become a force to be reckoned with and anyone who was an enemy of Imogen was to them something worth fighting for. And Mavis was vocal in her pain. "No one pulls the wool twice on this old girl," she told Kay. "She led me up the canal with her stupid star quality talk. If I had star quality it would be on that video for all to see, not hidden behind her flat-chested, flat stomach jumping jacks." And Kay agreed with her.

I told Mavis she was overreacting, letting her feelings for Imogen get in the way of reason. What had Martin's interest in Rodger's exhibition got to do with the Bag lady?

Mavis looked at me with an *isn't it obvious* look, "The shed," she said, "holds most of his paintings." *Like I didn't know that.* "And you have *herself* in your back yard lighting fires. What if something happened?"

What was she on about?

Mavis looked at me, as did those in the queue, apart from two children wearing earplugs plugged into some sort of music that even I didn't want to hear.

"She's not a pyromaniac," I said. "She is a homeless woman who has no idea of how to sing."

"I know that," said Mavis. "But you need to do something soon as Martin is having a hernia, which makes him not only unpleasant to work for but determined, and what Martin wants Imogen delivers."

I muttered 'thanks', with a sinking feeling; Imogen was a threat, after all look what she did to me and look how she recovered from the Gala day.

A week after the Gala day Imogen had made it onto the front page of *The Squeak* and every other local paper from Dunoon to Mull with a picture that made her look the exact opposite of the swearing, ambitious, egomaniac that she was.

Under the heading: "No Swansong for the Zumba Ladies" was a photograph of Imogen sitting in front of the public toilets wrapped in a tin foil blanket, and behind her was a goose victoriously clutching half an egg roll in his beak. Imogen looked windswept and interesting with the sort of doe-eyed smile that would make any man change her flat tyre, even in the rain.

For a moment even I almost felt sorry for her... until I read about the ex-fireman who would not be participating in next year's show – apparently she had made a complaint. While other people found an arthritic pensioner demonstrating the ancient art of putting out a fire in slow motion entertaining, she found it 'detrimental to the safety of the community'. And there was not one mention in the article of a way too big, egomaniac poster, just more waffle about geese, swans and their ability to cause grievous bodily harm.

At least the fireman's heart was in the right place.

Imogen had managed to get rid of an established part of the Gala day for years, the ex-fireman. Nobody had ever complained before, but she had shamed him; what could she do to the Bag Lady that half the town were already moaning about?

Mavis grabbed my arm. "Lumpy says they are going to contact the Social... to sort her out, find her a home."

I told Mavis that she didn't need sorting out, that she was fine as she was, and Puss and I liked it that way. But Mavis wasn't convinced, and once Mavis told me about Imogen's new job, neither was I. Imogen, as far as I knew, worked for the council part time answering the phone, until her Zumba and her other artistic pursuits took off. I had no idea until Mavis pointed out that she now worked for the housing department. "Yes," said Mavis, "according to Martin the interview was a breeze."

"So what," I said, with my best brave face.

I was starting to get that panicky sick feeling again...just like in the hospital.

Mavis looked concerned, her newly waxed upper lip twitching as she pulled me closer to the bench. "And folk are talking; they say she's the reason for all that Gala day nonsense. It's serious, if the Social have their way she could be moved...anywhere."

"Those geese," said someone from the back. "They're dangerous, they can break an arm, you know!"

"Don't be ridiculous," Mavis said. "That's swans, not geese, and the only thing those swans are likely to break is a week-old French stick, and that's only if herself stops feeding them." Mavis looked at me. "I am fed up to the back teeth hearing about the Goose Lady. Ever since Chubby's article in the paper, that is all anyone seems to talk about, arm-breaking birds."

Mavis's passion took me by surprise...

"Martin, he has influence," said Mavis, "and he wants her away." She pulled out one of the petitions. "He wants me to fill this with signatures."

I looked at it. "Homeless people need homes, not shop fronts to sing in and not wild geese as pets."

Betty had warned me about the Bag Lady petition, and I thought she was exaggerating. I thought she'd just been at the half-price vodka again. She said that there was already two pages filled at Chubby's, and I had been too scared to look. *Imagine the Bag Lady with a hand held shower and an upright Hoover, just didn't seem right.*

"What are they going to do?" I said feebly, "fine her?"

Chapter Twenty-Three

THE SCRAPBOOK

Scratching an itch doesn't make it go away.

When the Bag Lady first handed me the scrapbook I was bemused, especially when she told me to 'add Beryl and others will follow'. But I knew it was something special and so I put the scrapbook in the safest place possible, my underwear drawer. At first I wrapped it in plastic. Then as I began to appreciate the uniqueness of such a book, I gave it a more attractive box.

It was a massive book, full of scraps of paper and photographs.

Reading the scrapbook had become part of our sitting by the fire ritual, and it had opened our eyes to another woman; it was full of stories and letters from Deirdre McConical, an agony aunt and columnist in a '70s magazine called *Fabulous You*.

Her stories were of heartache, sadness and sorrow. As for her advice, it was priceless. People wrote to her about their problems – husbands lost to younger women, wives disappearing into the sunset with the family car and lonely, angry people – and all were soothed by her special type of wisdom.

Her letters were always worth a second read. They were original, witty and, as Kay liked to put it, 'as surreal as Mary Poppins on hash!'

Every night, I went to bed, opened the tea-stained scrapbook at random, read one page, dreamt about it and then, in the morning along with my coffee in bed, I reread the story until I heard the Bag Lady singing. Then my coffee in bed switched to stewed tea by the fire, her cackle and Puss purring.

Most of all her stories inspired me, and as I walked back from Mavis and the post office I started to think about them, hoping for inspiration. Mavis had scared me. I had never seen her so animated.

I walked into the front door and looked at my mail; Rodger and Shifty had wanted to hold a custody meeting in the Argyll. They wanted to talk about the great divide and, as I refused to answer any text or phone messages or any of their notes, an official letter appeared; I read it, and poured a drink.

Rodger was winning, Imogen was winning, even Shifty was winning and Rodger by the tone of his letter knew it. He wanted to sell everything from the shed full of grotesque male thighs to the depressing landscape as well as our house and the shop. Dreams of revenge were slipping further from my grasp, along with everything else Rodger and I had together.

And now Rodger and Shifty, the upwardly mobile barman, wanted to take the Bag Lady from me too, my pal and her socks, her stories and her rotten stewed tea – my sole purpose for getting up in the morning.

Rodger's letter said that the Bag Lady and her campfires couldn't stay. It was all about protecting the assets. And nothing was to be touched. Any revenge would be met with revenge. And I knew whose idea it was, because, despite his love of tofu, Shifty was a man of aggression. I saw what he did to his ex. She left the town with nothing but her wok, a bag full of Lycra and of course the instructor. She was stripped of any chance of working in a community centre from here to John O' Groats, thanks to Shifty and his network. Shifty knew people and now with Imogen on his side he was a force to be reckoned with.

I was beginning to feel anxious, this new Rodger was hard to deal with, and how was I supposed to react?

Every time I thought of my pal under the Social, on some housing association estate, my panic attacks lurched into action. No more fires, no more Puss in the tent, no more light in the garden for me to look out on, no more horrible tea.

It was another Sheryl moment and I called her.

Sheryl was not impressed; "why do you keep turning to me and then ignoring my advice?" she said on the phone, so I offered her a drink.

At first Rodger wanted the shed, the keys to the shed and all that was in the shed. He claimed that he had built, bought and paid for the shed and all that was in it, so it was his. Sheryl had called it a "perfectly reasonable request stating that as they were his paintings he should have them." At the time I called her pedantic, which I now regret.

Sheryl read Rodger's latest and looked up with an *I told you so* look.

She then went to the bin, and pulled an older more 'reasonable' note and pressed it flat on her lap like a piece of a treasure map. She was talking about the importance of moving on and how I had to address the now. I didn't care for her tone, it was almost Kay-like, especially when she said, "if only you had listened, agreed to the shed."

I wondered if things weren't so rosy on the Steven front. Maybe there were problems and that's why she was so Kay-like. So bossy, I was beginning to regret asking her around, she even refused a drink. Instead she sat down on the floor and started pulling out all the other notes from the bin that Puss had missed. "You need to keep all these," she said, "and start focusing."

I felt like a child standing in front of her parents as they silently read a bad school report. I was beginning to miss my happy pal.

"They really wanted the shed, didn't they?" she muttered. "If only you'd given it to them."

More if onlys!

I wanted to pull the notes from her and shove them back into the bin, but I knew despite her nagging, Sheryl was right.

That night I contacted Rodger. "I'll meet you at the Calarden," I texted, "on Sunday and we can talk". I wanted to meet somewhere away from Lochgilphead, somewhere neutral and inhibiting for Rodger. I knew he would bring Shifty and I wanted some advantage.

The Calarden was a small pub in a back street in Oban. On Sunday, at lunchtime, it had karaoke along with a free children's meal with each roast. No one I knew went there; it was the perfect place; definitely no hand holding.

Chapter Twenty-Four

THE SUMMIT

Gyration Is The Lowest Form Of Dance.

So there I was sitting on a used newspaper on the edge of my seat in the darkest corner of The Calarden wondering when it had gone so downmarket. Last time I was at the Calarden there was a bus party, and a meat buffet. Now you were lucky to get a choice of crisps, and the only music playing was from the slot machines lined up near the Gents.

I was sitting on a newspaper because the seat had that sticky feel to it. God knows what made it sticky, but I didn't want it on my best attire. I wanted to make Rodger realise that the Neff was still a force to be missed. I had my hair straightened in a Cleopatra bob, and wore a red top which floated around the midriff, a black leather jacket and jeans. Jeans always work in a 'good for your age, young at heart' look; well, to anyone who was around in the '70s, that is. And of course leather says don't mess with me unless you want trouble.

There were two bouncers at the door with shaven heads, white t-shirts and way too tight jeans, reminding me of EastEnders goes to the gym. They stood with a 'you're dead if you look the wrong way' expressions with their hands crossed across their crotch. As if anyone wanted to go there!

I had arrived early, which was not my idea. Sheryl wanted to get to the shops for some bread and cheese, and dropped me off with an 'I'll not take too long' promise. It was a Sunday lunchtime, and there was not one mouth with a full set of teeth to be found in the bar. Even the barman, who was as ancient as the '70s deco and beer-soaked beer mats, smiled with gaps. Greasy hair was the norm and as time went on it was clear that I was the only one sober apart from the two bouncers at the door.

Then a drunken man half my age sauntered up to my table and flopped beside me with a 'how's it hanging?'. I was working on a comment when from behind I heard "Bugger arf. She's waiting for someone and it's no you."

The drunk eyed me and then glared at the ash-blonde woman. He downed his pint, slammed it on the table and staggered off or 'arf' as the drunk would say. Miss Ash-blonde eyed me up and down and then sat beside me. "You're waiting for someone, aren't you?"

I gave her my 'what's it to you' look with as much of a casual air as I could muster.

She winked with a mysterious air and then offered me a real drink, and as the feeling of unease began to increase I suggested a whisky.

"A large," she said to the barman. "She looks like she needs it." And then she stood by me waiting for the money. Turns out she was the barman's daughter with a facial tick. She told me she remembered me with a cryptic tilt of her glasses. "Don't know where," she said, "but it'll come to me."

I had no idea who she was.

Rodger was wheeled in by Shifty. His plastered ankle caught one of the old ladies sitting by the door. She was half cut and completely oblivious to the fact that he was in plaster. She threw him a glare accompanied by suitable verbal abuse. Which Rodger chose to ignore.

Then I watched Rodger knock over a glass and grimace in pain. The pub was full by then and everyone stopped and stared. Even the two knuckleheads, who I am sure, if Rodger looked the wrong way, would've had him out of the door before you could shout 'it's a raid'. Shifty wheeled him to my table and then took a seat.

"Why on earth did you choose here?" said Shifty. "I mean, the

Calarden is not the sort of place you spill other people's drinks in, not if you want to leave with your nose intact."

I smiled. *Maybe it'll be alright after all, point one to me!*

I looked into Rodger's eyes. Rodger's hair had grown and his mouth was not so rigid. His eyebrows were still visible but less prominent thanks to a longer fringe. He was just a foot away from me, the closest we had sat together since the hospital. I stared into his dark eyes and the familiar feelings in my stomach began to stir. Rodger looked back with the odd grimace. Nearly every time someone staggered by, some part of Rodger's body was knocked, followed by a 'sorry, mate.' I was beginning to feel sympathy for him.

Shifty ordered the drinks. "Diet coke for me," he said.

"Aye, and me too," muttered Rodger.

"And whatever she's having," said Shifty.

I lifted my glass. "I'll have a refill."

Shifty turned up his nose with an 'I gather Sheryl's coming back,' comment, which I chose to ignore.

Point two to me!

Rodger looked into my eyes and all the past few months melted. I saw what I used to see, what I sometimes still remember. Then he motioned me to come closer. I put my head towards his lips and felt his breath on my neck. The world stopped for a moment and his warm lips almost touched my skin.

He whispered, "Codpiece."

"What?"

"You can have the codpiece."

I leant back in my seat. "Are you trying to be funny?"

"You need it more than me; I am finished with it." *Which I found quite hurtful, there was a time when that codpiece gave us both a lot of pleasure.*

I looked at Rodger; his eyebrows tilted in his familiar cryptic fashion and I cleared my whisky in a gulp.

"What the hell is that supposed to mean, I need it more than you?"

"It's a figure of speech," said Shifty, "what with you liking the theatre, performing and all that. Maybe you could use it, we both agreed!"

They both agreed, on my stuff? Point one to the opposition.

The ash-blonde, who was now standing behind the bar, pointed at me like I had just lifted way too many beer mats and was going to make a run for it. Everybody looked as she began to tell the whole world and Oban how she saw me, perform at the old folks *do* in the Argyll.

"You're the plum pudding lady," she said, and turned to the rest of the bar. "She burst out of a plum pudding and 'lap danced', it was years ago."

"I have never lap danced in my life," I said.

But she wasn't listening, the ash-blonde had an audience to entertain, "I was just a kid, Granddad was playing the accordion, and she burst out of a plum pudding, in a sequin bra. Even when he was dying he talked about 'that bra'," she said. "Do you still have it?"

I threw her a 'could you tone it down a decibel' look and told her it was 'belly dancing', to which she replied 'same thing isn't it'.

I looked to Rodger and Shifty for some sort of support, after all they were there. They saw me belly dance, they saw Bingo the dog attack my bra, chewing it beyond recognition. In fact it was a night I would rather forget. It was one of my first gigs in the Argyll, dancing for the old folks' Christmas 'Do'. The idea was that I would surprise everyone with an entrance they would never forget. Rodger would set the plum pudding alight, I would jump out, and belly dance for them. And it would have worked too, except for Bingo the dog, who made a beeline for my bra and wouldn't let go.

Archie had, according to the barman, dined out on the Christmas do story for as long as anyone could remember. Apparently there was even a picture in the gents of Archie with Bingo on his knee, clutching my bra between his teeth.

"Bingo clung onto that bra for weeks," said the barman. "Chewing it, sleeping with it, dragging it around the Argyll like a mangled, Barbie doll."

Was I to be flattered or what?

"There is no lap dancing in belly dancing," I finally said to the ash-blonde, "and as for my underwear, I mean what idiot would keep a chewed-up bra covered in dog spit for a decade?"

"Belly dancer Lap dancers who pretend to be belly dancers," said the ash-blonde, and that's when Shifty along with Rodger began to snigger.

Typical. Life's one long big laugh when you're in love - point two to the opposition.

The meeting was not going well. Shifty and Rodger looked comfortable and relaxed while I, even with a few whiskies, was as tense as a cornered rabbit. In fact, that's how I felt, like a rabbit trapped under the lights of a seedy pub and the glazed eyes of its locals. So when the artist in a wheelchair and his handsome 'carer' began to talk about their paintings, the pub quietened down. It seemed like everyone wanted to know if the lap dancer with the Egyptian haircut was going to let the nice couple have their paintings for their show. Or was she going to make life difficult?

"They are safe in the shed," I finally muttered.

Rodger was letting this barman do all the talking. A barman whose idea of culture came out of a yogurt pot; a barman who had ruined my life. Why was he doing all the talking? So Rodger's jaw was in a bad state, but he should still be able to mumble for himself, shouldn't he?

"Can he not speak for himself?" I finally said.

Rodger looked at me in pain while Shifty glared. "Are you stupid? Look at his jaw."

Apparently life with a wired jaw was no picnic, as the ash-blonde pointed out along with a few 'hear hears' from the others.

We were fighting over everything, all the things we used to share, from the slow cooker to the toothbrush holder. And my only dream was to make sure that I got the slow cooker, along with everything else that I didn't use, but he wanted.

Then when I mentioned the Bag Lady's human right to fry fish outside in my garden, Rodger nearly choked on his straw. Suddenly he started talking and Shifty couldn't get a word in.

Shifty tried to calm him down and began to waffle on about the Social being aware. But Rodger was having none of it. "What do you see in her? Why do you care, you care more for her and her lice-ridden, flee-bitten squalor than you ever did me, why? I did everything for you," Rodger huffed. "I bet she don't change your CDs. Bet she don't prance for you in a codpiece."

Shifty told him to be quiet, but he was on a roll.

"You were so loved up about your flexible hips and goddess shit that you never noticed me and now here you are giving it all up for a geese-feeding bag lady who will probably bugger off once she's cleared you out of padded bras and sequins."

"I don't wear padded bras."

"She doesn't, I can vouch for that," said ash-blonde.

"Did it ever occur to you," continued Rodger, "that I might like a little attention?"

"Like Shifty and his posing?"

The whole pub was silent now, everyone was watching except for an old lady in the corner talking to her Jack Russell. "There you go, ole fellar, salt and vinegar, your favourite," she looked at me. "Aye, a woman should love her man or he'll look elsewhere for his salt and vinegar," she muttered, as Ole Fellar let out a bark.

Shifty wheeled Rodger through the crowd, which had parted like Moses and the Red Sea. The day had not gone as I imagined. The salt and vinegar lady recognised Rodger from the local paper and asked him to sign a few beer mats and then handed them around in exchange for free drinks. Then Shifty started talking about the up and coming exhibition and how he could do a deal on cheap prints.

I may as well have been a toilet roll in the Gents for all they cared; even the aging barman who had been calling me the exotic dancer dropped his interest once he heard about Rodger's Frontal Winds exhibition. "What the hell kind of name is that?" he asked, and Shifty's cryptic response was "come and see", leaving business cards on the table.

A business card, in the Calarden?

After the happy couple left I pulled up a stool at the bar. The young drunk returned, fumbled onto the seat next to me, and offered me a crisp. "You're better off without your bra," he slurred, then slid off his stool, like jelly off a plate.

I stared out to the entrance of the pub. It had stopped raining, the sun had come out and a misty haze was forming. The door opened and Sheryl appeared with her red hair framed by the setting sun. For a moment she looked like an angel clutching a Tesco bag.

"Sorry I'm late," she said. "There was a queue at the checkout."

Chapter Twenty-Five

SLOE GIN

There is a time for lighting and a time for putting out a fire and that is not the same time.

Imogen came to my house; apparently she stood at the front door and knocked and when no one answered, she came around the back "where all the noise was coming from".

She pushed open the side gate and ploughed through the muddy drive in her heeled leather boots and came across Betty, the Bag Lady, Mavis, and Iona along with yours truly sitting by the fire. We were all laughing as Betty read from the scrapbook. Imogen stood at the edge of the lawn, slim and elegant despite the flick marks of mud on her shoes and skirt, waiting for someone to notice her.

"Dear Deidre," read Betty.

"Hello," shouted Imogen.

No one answered, we didn't even look up as Betty continued to read, and Imogen shouted "hello" again.

Imogen, unfazed, walked over to the fire and sat on a spare log like she was part of the group. Ignoring the fact that she was being ignored, she asked what we were reading; Betty continued...

Dear Artful Dodger,

I have not printed your letter as I feel the names of body parts used out of context are inappropriate for readers of this page. But let me just reiterate. I did not suggest that to overcome your obsession with stealing, you should adopt a Robin Hood stance.

Please stop handing out PlayStations nicked from Oxfam shops to children in the park, no matter how bureaucratic you think Oxfam has become. It is not legal. And please stop handing out sex manuals to the Seventh Day Adventist. It's not funny; and as far as I am aware they are still capable of having sexual relations without any instruction.

Betty closed the book as we all laughed, apart from Imogen. "I don't understand," she said.

"It is what you want it to be," said Betty, emulating the Bag Lady.

"Deirdre then, is she someone I should know?" Imogen continued, ignoring the laughter, "is she?"

"No," said the Bag Lady, who took the book from Betty and slid it into her tee pee.

"Oh," Imogen flashed a smile; "did you not get my note? The council have asked me to visit you?"

Imogen looked from one face to another.

It was three o'clock in the afternoon I had shut the shop, Betty had made her excuses from the Argyll Hotel kitchen, Iona had organised someone else to feed her horses and Mavis had thrown a sickie. We were all here because of Imogen's stupid *I have arranged to visit you on (Date inserted) at (time inserted), you may have someone present* letter.

How were we to know that she'd arrive early, catching us off guard?"

"Why do you think we are all here?" Mavis finally said.

Imogen, still unfazed and now in teacher (her), child (us) mode, began to explain that she had "forms to fill." "We need to know all about you, so we can apply for a house - I mean you can't live like this, can you?" She waited for a response, and when none came asked if it was necessary for all of us to be there, and when the Bag Lady answered with a robust "yes!" Imogen, still unfazed, carried on.

She pulled out a form as thick as a doorstop, and a *your needs are our promises* council pen from her leather satchel, as Betty in an effort to unnerve the opposition said, "thought you just answered phones for the council."

"And organised Prance and Pose days," muttered Mavis.

Imogen still *unnerved* told us that this was her "new position" *as opposed to a new job*, "I used to work for the Social," she said, "years ago and Martin thought it would be a good idea for me to get back on the bike - as he liked to put it." We looked at her. "I am a trained social worker, you know."

"A force to be reckoned with," muttered Betty.

"I am here to help," she said, flashing her perfect teeth.

The Bag Lady, before anyone had a chance to defend, asked, "why?"

"No one wants to live like this." She gestured to my garden. "I mean I am sure Neff here is trying to help;" she looked at the others, "I am sure you all are, but a shed full of paintings is hardly a home, let alone a tent."

"Tee pee," said the Bag Lady.

And then Imogen mentioned the petition, and before she had time to pull it out, Betty jumped in. "There are plenty of people who didn't sign; who like things as they are."

Imogen let out a sigh, and stared at the tee pee with all its glorious decorations; decorations that the Bag Lady had collected from her walks and geese feeding. There was a sheep's skull on the top of the tee pee, covered in broken bits of pottery and glass which Puss sniffed at now and then. And at the door, like a welcome mat, was a rubber bath mat, pink and curling at the edges.

"That is my home," said the Bag Lady. "It has seen me through storms and the frost."

"It's a tent," said Imogen, "completely unsuitable for living in."

"Tell that to a native American," said Iona.

"We are not in America," said Imogen, "and this is just a makeshift shelter for children to play in."

Iona by now was looking angry and started to talk about how the tee pee wasn't makeshift at all, *although it could do with a little bleach.* Iona stated that a tee pee was a recognised living space for many indigenous people and that for centuries wars had been fought and lost with societies living in tee pees. "Look at the Mongols," she said, "look at the Inuit, must we completely bow to conservatism?"

"Hear, hear," shouted Betty.

Imogen began to shuffle her papers, trying to balance them on her satchel, and suggested that we start with a date of birth and address.

Then Mavis talked about the artist within. "I mean look at this place," she said as she gestured to the skull balancing against all odds on the tip of the tee pee. "Every night I come here to find trinkets from nowhere, worthless treasures that have been raised to a new level of art form," said Mavis.

"Recycling," chipped in Iona.

"And more," said Mavis, "A place worthy of a campfire and to quote Nefertiti herself, for goddess dancing."

"Hear, hear," said Betty.

"And," continued Mavis, now on a roll, "The Bag lady has befriended a lonely woman, heart broken and dumped like a used teabag. She," said Mavis gesturing to the Bag Lady, "has given her," gesturing to me, "someone to come home to."

"Hear, hear," said everyone but me.

Imogen was no longer unfazed; instead she looked uncomfortable, twirling her pen between her fingers, wondering *I would think*, about what she had walked into.

"Where were you born?" she finally asked and like all of us waited for an answer; everyone wanted to know the Bag Lady's story. But none came; instead the Bag Lady stood up and began to rearrange the clump of crow feathers attached to the skull, pulled a few wilting nettles from the entrance, then started to untangle the string of *wind chime* shells rattling in the breeze.

I had forgotten that the Bag Lady never answered a question with any sense, if at all and for the first time wondered if Imogen was out of her depth.

Imogen's discomfort grew, but she ploughed on and for the next hour, asked questions, and got nowhere. Any question she asked the Bag Lady, the Bag Lady had no answer to. She had no previous address apart from the tee pee, her birthday was for her to remember when she felt like it, and as for a name - who needed a name when everyone knew her as the Bag Lady?

"But I can't put that on a form," snapped Imogen, exasperated and out of her comfort zone.

The Bag Lady with the face of boredom adjusted the curl in the bath mat, pulled a dandelion from the grass and tickled Puss's ear, tormenting her until she played.

Imogen's power stance had diminished; an hour ago she was sitting on a log like she owned it, now she looked like she wished the ground would swallow her up, along with the log and her empty forms. While we, the *let's save the Bag Lady* group sat redundant, we had given up our afternoon to protect her, she who needed no protection.

Finally out of sympathy and because it was after five o'clock, I offered Imogen a homebrew. I went to Rodger's secret stash of sloe gin under the stairs, and poured us all one. Imogen, after mumbling something about being out of practice, insisted on a spritzer. Three glasses later, Imogen shouted, "forget the soda water" and was sculling it straight.

Imogen not only claimed that she was out of practice but that since Martin had taken the pledge, she found it hard to relax. "And now with this new job," she muttered, "I feel as tight as a spring, my massage therapist says I have knots like a fishing line, impossible to untangle."

"Which means," said Mavis, "more treatments."

"Although the interview was a 'breeze'," continued Imogen, "the job itself is anything but - I mean this is my first visit and no one has even shown me the ropes."

Betty muttered an "obvious."

"The office is always empty," she said with a slight slur.

"That's the council for you," said Iona.

"It's all Martin's idea, the last thing I want to do is fill out forms, I am an artist, helping women. You understand don't you, Naff; sorry, Neff?"

Not exactly a health and safety comment.

"I mean look at this." She pulled out her form, half of which cascaded on to the ground. "I finished training years ago, nothing I learnt translates into this, bloody Martin and his 'get back on the bike' ideas." She emptied her glass in one gulp. "God I need to chill," she said, handing me an empty glass for more.

As Imogen began to *chill*, the girls became agitated, Imogen was full of her own stories and it was clear that she had no intention of leaving. Betty, Mavis and Iona, having tasted Rodger's homebrew before took it slowly; the last person they wanted to be stuck with half cut was "her". In fact they now began to make *time to go* hints that Imogen didn't pick up and the look on their face was relief. I could tell not one of them wanted the task of taking her home, they were packing up with a speed I had rarely seen, even in a January sale.

Imogen became so relaxed she tucked whatever was left of her forms back into the satchel and let Puss onto her lap with a reminiscent look. *Puss didn't stay long.* Maybe it was the shadows of the fire flickering, the outlines of trees lit up by the moon or the smell of magnolias slowly overpowering the smell of the Bag Lady's fried fish. I had no idea, but Imogen seemed planted by the fire for the night and had begun to be all whimsical and poetic. Not a pretty sight, as she had an educated high-pitched voice, and a smile which started and ended at her lips. She had as much ability to hold an audience as a passport officer, talking in another language. And that audience was now three, if you counted Puss.

Betty, Mavis and Iona had made their escape; they disappeared into the house and never returned, leaving me with Imogen talking about Martin and his love for the council.

"How can a person change so rapidly?" she said, as I watched Iona's back disappearing into the kitchen. "There is not an artistic thought in his head these days. It is all money and the lack of it."

I saw my night pan out before me, stuck with a woman I hated, the sort of woman that no amount of alcohol made bearable. Imogen, banging on about her mission to enlighten the women of Argyll with rhythm and how Martin was more into taxable deductions than watching her dance.

"Martin used to pick out my Lycra for me," she said "I used to parade before him bouncing along to Ricky Martin; now he'd rather listen to the *Money Programme*."

Not exactly something you want to hear over a pile of council paper fluttering in the wind. I began to pick them up.

"Everything in its place," the Bag lady said, while tipping her tea into a saucer for Puss to drink; she too was packing up and making *time for bed* noises.

Imogen, who was watching me retrieve the last of papers, shouted, "you're absolutely right, everything in its frigging place," grabbed the papers and with the flare of a magician scattering cards into the air, tossed them into the fire. A dramatic action which none of us took seriously, *there was plenty more in the office.*

The papers caught by the breeze flew everywhere; some landed by Puss, she blinked unmoved, others landed in her tea, and she stood up and stretched, while others fluttered onto the fire. The Bag Lady, noting that Puss had no interest in her cold tea, *like every other night* poured it into the now smothered fire, which let out a half-hearted hiss.

"Before I met Martin, I was a flower bud, waiting to unfold," said Imogen with dewy eyes. "There were no half measures with my Martin. He was a man who was as quiet in public as he was flamboyant in private. He was a man who loved red and blue together, who liked chocolate and whisky at the same time, and who liked me in the morning as well as at night. Now, all he cares about is his precious accountant."

Like I said, not a pretty sight; the Bag Lady began to rattle her dishes under the outside tap just beside the shed. While Imogen, fired up by the sloe gin, began to cry, as she pulled a tissue from somewhere and dabbed her eyes.

"This is why I don't drink..." she blubbered.

"This is not the time for crying," the Bag Lady said, as she stashed her dishes in the trolley by the shed. Then she pulled her blanket off the ground and began to shake it so vigorously that I started to splutter from the dust, along with Puss.

"It's socks time," said the Bag Lady, placing her blanket on top of the dishes in the trolley. Then she threw the rest of Imogen's sloe gin onto the fire, despite my claims that it was liquid gold; the fire gave out a final hiss and died.

"His jewels are locked up for the winter," a tearful Imogen moaned.

The Bag Lady wasn't even listening; she was humming, engrossed in her getting to bed ritual. She crawled into her tee pee, pulled a couple of odd socks from her bag, flicked them open and pulled them on, oblivious to the holes in the heels. Puss threw herself into a stretch, shook off the dust and then disappeared into the tee pee without even a glance at yours truly.

I took Imogen's glass and began to guide her into the house, "Not that his jewels were anything extraordinary," Imogen whispered into my ear. "But he knew what to do with them; hard to imagine I know, but you know what they say about bald men."

Not that I ever found out, for as soon as Imogen collapsed on the couch she fell asleep snoring...

I pulled a blanket over her, and texted Martin from her phone. I looked at my enemy; the woman who had taken all my students without a thought. Even asleep, half comatose with the slow rumble of a snore she looked glamourous. Her blonde ponytail was seductively ruffled, and her makeup barely smudged, you would hardly know she'd been blubbering.

Imogen had spent the whole night talking about a small round man whose Wee Bit of Art shop was leaking money. A man that had sent her back to work in a *position* she hated, so that his shop could continue to lose money; while she dreamed of conquering Argyll with armies of women "giving their all" in pink Lycra.

"You understand, don't you, Neff, you had it once, (*I liked to think I still had it*), I am what you were, except so much better."

Cheers.

"Martin says I've gone too far. I want too much." *I was beginning to feel for Martin.*

Imogen talked about recognition. She wanted *along with everything else,* her Zumba work to be seen for what it was, liberating woman from themselves.

"It's a dance," I said.

She didn't hear, instead she continued on about being recognised. "I want my picture on the Wall of Gratitude, if Sheila the yoga teacher is up there, why shouldn't I be?" she said, she even knew what she wanted written underneath, *the teacher that brought dance into the twentieth century*. "I want my face to be there long after I have gone," she said, "for an eternity", or *at least until the council build a new community centre.*

And Martin called her greedy.

Imogen was all me, me, me, and it was boring even with a few sloe gins and by the light of a campfire. She bored the Bag Lady into silence and Betty into leaving early, Betty who loved to sit all hours by the fire and didn't like going home.

I tucked the blanket around her, as she snored into my purple sequined cushion, an ancient present from Rodger. *If anyone deserved a picture of themselves eternally sandwiched between Sheila and Lumpy's photo, it was definitely her.*

Chapter Twenty-Six

GETTING EVEN

Salute the sun and be free in your thoughts, but remember to keep them to yourself.

Imogen woke up looking just as she did the night before; fresh, no puffy eyes and just enough smudged mascara to look seductive. With a quick ruffle of her hair, her ponytail was straightened and with a quick dap of a wet tissue her makeup was sorted. I gave her a coffee and immediately hated her again.

I woke up thinking about Imogen's *you are like me* comment. It was a depressing moment that even a coffee wouldn't lighten. Imogen had bored the backside off everyone about dance, the joy of rhythm and changing the face of Argyll. She had cleared the camp fire quicker than a gas leak with rants about Martin. Her ego was as massive as, it seems Martin's tax bill. And I realised that I had not only been listening to Imogen but to myself, looking at myself drunk and annoyingly loud, only with better makeup.

Was she right; was I that bad, was I more like Imogen than not? Would the Bag Lady be better off under the Social, and the world a better place with a view of Rodger's 'Frontal Winds'? No wonder I was alone, no wonder Puss preferred the tee pee and its feet-like aromas to my bed.

I walked into the sitting room still in my dressing gown with two cups of coffee, and there she stood, blankets folded and looking through my Rodger notes, laughing.

"He does have a sense of humour, doesn't he?" she said.

"Do you think so?"

"Yes, I mean, he is joking with all these threats - isn't he?"

"Well, they are not exactly threats," I said, taking the notes from her along with my best "none of your business" look.

"But he talks about wrapping a pound of mince around your beads and feeding them to the dog," Imogen said.

"He's speaking more - metaphorically, that dog isn't here anymore."

"Shoving your dance CDs down a sewage pipe?"

"That's just talk, I mean Rodger has no idea about pipes." I was trying to put her off, explain that Rodger was all mouth, and the more she painted him as the enemy, the more I wanted to shut her up.

But Imogen didn't listen; she was as passionate about "getting what you're due" as she was about Zumba. "You have to grab all you can," she said, and then with a scathing look at my dressing gown added, "I mean you're not young, it's not like you have many chances left."

"What's that supposed to mean?"

"Take those paintings," she said, waving her hand in the general direction of the shed. "You're entitled to half."

"I'm sleeping alone with not even a cat on my bed," I said. "No amount of paintings is going to make that better."

"You never know, they could be worth something."

"What, abstract penises, who would pay to hang that on the wall?"

Imogen muttered something about one man's meat and started to lecture me about divorce again; launching into her multiple settlements like they were business deals.

"Divorce is tricky," she said. "You can lose everything, believe me, divorce is all about who gets what, and if you are not quick, that bastard will get it all. You have to play dirty, dirtier than him. My first was a disaster, I walked out with a pair of flip flops and my coffee machine, not much use, but I learnt. Three years of cleaning swimming pools and windows is a great teacher." She looked at me, slumped in my dressing gown; "a settlement is your best friend and, at your age, probably your only one."

I suggested that she should leave, but she was not listening. "You need to protect yourself and your future, and helping that Bag Lady isn't one of them. You need a better plan. Or I should say a plan, rather than ignoring these messages and threats." She pulled a few of the notes from my hand and tossed them into the air, *dramatic - way over the top.* "You need to outsmart him."

I told her, *while picking up the notes,* that Rodger and I weren't exactly married, and Imogen exploded.

"What's that got to do with it? You've been together for over ten years, your best years, why should he call all the shots? In fact you should talk to Martin, get him to help you, he is as ruthless as they come."

I told her that everything was up for sale, the house, and the shop.

"Oh that's right, Martin helped Rodger, forgot about that," Imogen sighed, sniffed at her coffee, pulled a face and then sipped it, like a child taking medicine. Her hangover, it seemed, had arrived.

Imogen had exhausted me, sucked me dry, she had talked about buyouts and sellouts. She told me to keep copies of everything and make a note of what I needed "just to get by". I finally retreated into the kitchen hoping that maybe, if I started to feed Puss she would shut up, or even leave. But she didn't, she followed me, talking at high speed about lawyers and how she'd been through a few.

"I can smell a good yin a mile off," she said while dumping my Tesco's finest Italian blend down the sink. *I may as well have given her a Nescafé.*

Imogen washed her cup out, filled it with water and downed it in three gulps, "What is it you want?" she said, wiping her mouth with a small belch. "Because if you don't know, it will be taken from you before you do."

Chapter Twenty-Seven

THE CARRY OUT

A friend in need is just a chancer

After Imogen's sermon, I went to the book shop. I felt sick and lethargic in a sort of low key way. I plonked myself onto the couch.

I had been working at the shop every day since Rodger's accident and I had come to enjoy it. The place was starting to feel like mine, especially once all the shed posters were gone. And it grieved me to think about losing it.

I had spent the day serving customers in the morning and listening to the Bag Lady and Betty in the afternoon, occasionally flicking through a self-help book. Betty had become a regular visitor not only to the tee pee, but also outside the shop, where she sat on a stool during the Bag Lady's many coffee breaks.

The Bag Lady often retreated into a world of her own and Betty, it seemed, wanted to be part of that world. Betty thought that the Bag Lady could communicate with the dead, specifically her Duncan. She took the Bag Lady's quotes as future reading, and her singing as some sort of meditative chant, when in fact the Bag Lady was just singing made-up words to Beatle songs, with the odd mixed up quotes from her scrapbook. All of which was inspired by stewed tea at the fire or coffee and toffee outside the shop. When the Bag Lady told Betty about Martin's Wee Bit of Art shop going under, Betty saw this as confirmation, despite the fact that it was Imogen who told everyone the night before. Betty, like Iona and Mavis, was too focused on escaping to hear.

"How did she know?" said Betty during one of her trips into the back room to make more coffee. "Shifty, said to "keep it under your hat", that they were hoping that Rodger's exhibition would put the Wee Bit of Art shop back on its feet."

"Imogen," I muttered, but Betty wasn't listening. She was walking out of the shop with a determined look on a par with Kay, who had just arrived. They grunted at each other.

Betty and the Bag Lady were having their standard argument about tea leaves. Betty had taken to tipping the Bag Lady's half-drunk tea onto the fire and handing the empty cup to the Bag Lady for a psychic reading. And the Bag Lady was now explaining to Mavis, yet again, how it was only Mavis's tea leaves that told Mavis's future and that she had never read a tea leaf in her life.

And Kay didn't seem to hear a word; she was like a woman with something big on her mind. "We need to do something," she said.

The Bag Lady and Betty continued to argue.

"I told you, it is your teacup we read, not mine," the Bag Lady sniffed. "And if it is not finished it can't be read, you cannot chuck half a cup of tea on the fire and expect to see your future."

"Aye, but that tosser took advantage of me even after he died; in his will he said that he was right and I was wrong," said Betty. "And I want to put it right!"

Kay looked around at the empty shop. "I'm telling you this is serious."

"What is the point of poking about like some vulture over a carcass?" said the Bag Lady. "If he disagreed in life he will disagree in death, ghosts are like leopards, they don't change their marks!"

"Spots!"

"Marks!"

"What would you know?" Shouted Betty.

Kay gestured to the two outside. "Have you seen the paper?"

I shook my head.

"She's been feeding the birds from the Indian; and now anyone carrying a plastic bag is fair game, apparently the birds have got a taste for naans." Kay tossed the *Fyne News* onto the bench. "Read it."

"I see," I said, *assuming that "she" was the Bag lady.*

"The whole world is against her, making up stories that aren't true, that woman is as much a curry lover as you are a DIY expert. You need a plan or she'll be shipped out, sent to a one-bedroom flat in Campbeltown until she sets off one too many fire alarms. Then she'll be sedated for her own safety and God knows what will happen to her".

Kay had experience with the Social, and it had left her a little bitter and prone to exaggeration.

"I just want closure," said Betty.

"Don't we all," shouted Kay.

The Bag Lady, like she always did, told Mavis, that 'Closure had been hers for the taking all along'. Betty muttered a satisfied, "oh, yes you said that before didn't you?"

Kay looked at me I felt tired and drained with all that anger and "getting even" advice from Imogen. She had even given me a list of lawyers; had Rodger and I really come to that?

"You haven't given up have you?" she said.

Maybe a good dose of caffeine might help give me some ideas. According to Deirdre McConical, 'Peace leads to thought, clarity and vision and if, after a decent cup of tea, none comes, then source a friend. I looked at Kay, *maybe not.*

"You of all people, I always thought you had more − balls than most."

I looked at Kay with disbelief, I couldn't believe it...

"You've changed your tune." I said. "The last time I stupidly moaned to you, you were all for the Social. *"What will Puss do without the Bag Lady?"* I said to you *"She'll be unbearable. How can I cope with a depressed cat?"* and you called me selfish, *"the 'Bag Lady's needs came before a cat," you said, "she should be in out of the rain and centrally heated like the rest of us, she needs the Social, not you and your bloody cat'."*

"That's different," muttered Kay, "you were thinking about you, not her outside."

"I had even offered her my shed," I said.

"Oh for Christ sake it's a bloody shed and it's not even your shed and she is never gonna move into it, is she?"

Kay picked up a *Shed for Dummies book* from the 'buy one get one free' basket. "What are we going to do about her, she can't go to Campbeltown, we'll never see her?"

"Iona says it's a good idea", I said.

"What?"

"She said it's do-able, living in a shed."

"What would a horsewoman know about sheds," Kay said, and then realising how stupid that sounded, back tracked - "that's not what I meant".

I stared out the window; normally I had some sort of answer but my mind was blank. What a relief it was to see Mavis barging through the door with Lumpy at her rear. Mavis excelled in uncomfortable conversations – others' that is; she never seemed to read body language or pick up signals of irritations. A skill probably mastered from working in a post office by yourself, faced with a queue once too often.

They were carrying a selection of bags. Mavis with a 'you look like you don't eat much these days' sermon, began to unpack the bags in a Salvation Army sort of way; clearing the top of my desk, moving books and pads with a 'where does this go?' and putting papers in the bin with a 'do you want this?' and 'is this wrapper necessary?'

Then along with Lumpy they began to empty their bags, meticulously spreading out their bits and pieces in order of starters and main, followed by a reverent unwrapping of their homemade Indian.

Kay and I watched as they set to like a couple who had been together for years, Mavis constantly talking. It doesn't take long before you develop a deaf ear to Mavis and by the looks of Lumpy he had already developed one.

"Lumpy, don't forget the sauce; Lumpy, where's the napkins? Mind the desk, oh it's okay, darl, we can use these," said Mavis, pulling a roll of kitchen roll from under the desk like a lump of unexpected gold. "Mind the floor, darl; it's okay, I've got it, you get the desk. Where's the dhal? Did you bring it or was I supposed to?"

I said nothing. Watching a couple dance about an Indian spread was way better than listening to Kay tell me I had given up or, when she had gone, sitting in the dark with one of Rodger's shed pens for entertainment.

Mavis began to talk about how wonderful curry was when you're down. "It's like the promise of a new hope," she said. "A new coat, a new mind," and then she looked at Lumpy, "or a new man."

Kay rolled her eyes. She didn't do domestic bliss or, it seemed, a curry.

"And you," said Mavis, "need a new plan."

"New plan, she hasn't any, she's given up," said Kay.

"You need a strategic plan of negotiation," continued Mavis. "And Lumpy's your man; he didn't umpire the shinty games for nothing."

Mavis is a great lover of plans, and claims that they are indispensable when you are at a low. "There is nothing like fluttering through a book with pictures looking for something better, when you're down," she says. Mavis talked about false hope like it was an item on the menu, like a pair of shoes you just slapped on. Kay was growing impatient.

"Rodger's selling the shed," Kay said, "he is selling everything."

"I thought you didn't want the shed," said Mavis. "That it was taking up your pyramid space?"

"Just as I get used to things..." I muttered.

"Now you want the shed?" said Mavis. "Lumpy, now she wants the shed... Lumpy and I were going to help you fix the pyramid after the shed was gone, weren't we, Lumpy? And now you want the shed, what do you want the shed for? Why don't you do up the kitchen, with just a few bits of Blu-tack, laminated postcards and matching tea towels? It can really kid you into a good mood. Even just lining things up on a shelf in perfect order can lift a mood. As for polishing a sink..."

There was no point now, it was all going.

We all looked at the spread of food before us, as the street lamps had flickered on. I closed the shop and before Lumpy had a chance to offer both the Bag Lady and Betty any curry they had headed off talking about beauty spots, leopard marks and Imogen. For someone living in a tent, the Bag Lady had a strict routine and Betty, who had no routine whatsoever, had taken to following her.

"She doesn't really want the shed," said Kay. "She is, as I said, giving up."

"I am not giving up," I said. "The shed is still on the table."

Lumpy called the shed a symbol."

"Oh, of what? DIY? You've taken up DIY," said Mavis. "Is that because the belly dancing has gone tits up?"

"No," said Lumpy. "It's all about Rodger."

Kay and I exchanged looks. "About Rodger?"

Lumpy surprised us. He had always been a skinny annoying man with scratchy looking whiskers. Now clean-shaven and well fed, he was like a new person - a romantic philosopher. I was beginning to see that there was more to Lumpy than sweeping a floor; love had changed him. He talked of couples splitting amicably; remaining friends, he talked about the shed being a symbol of all that was Rodger and me, and that's why we couldn't let go.

"Solve the shed crisis," he said, "and everything will fall into place".

"It's a bloody shed," said Kay, "your logic, Lumpy, is completely hormonal, and as useless as your broom."

"I beg your pardon," said Mavis.

"Lumpy's broom," said Kay, "it has as much effect as a hair net on dust."

Mavis, clutching a pakora like a weapon, turned to me; "are you going to let your friend, talk about my Lumpy, in your shop like that?"

I slumped onto the couch, "I am tired," I muttered. . And for once I didn't care because all the fight in me had oozed out like jam in a donut squished in a toddler's hands. "I'm not bothered about winning anymore," I said. "I just want it all to go away."

Mavis sat next to me on one side and Kay the other. Kay's face softened.

"What you need is my Lumpy's help," Mavis said.

"A plan," Kay said.

"The key is knowing what you really want and what you will sacrifice for it," said Lumpy, "then you make Rodger think it is his idea. It's a way of winning without him knowing you're winning."

"Iona says that you can make a shed into a place to live," I muttered.

"The shed," said Kay, "I thought you wanted to cut it in half." And for the first time in what seemed ages we laughed.

Chapter Twenty-Eight

THE CHRISTMAS DO

Never turn your back on a friendly face; it may be the last you see.

The fire was dying down and so, it seemed, was the Bag Lady's patience with Betty.

She was winding down for the night and when she does she has no interest in listening and if not left alone she sings louder and louder like a child putting her fingers in her ears. She started to sing, she knew it annoyed Betty.

"Just my foot," Betty said. "That's all you see, after all that practice; my right bloody foot!"

"I thought it was your hand?"

"Mavis is livid, she says after all the support that her and Lumpy gave Imogen the least she could have done was give her a place to show off her toned stomach."

"Performing is not about the artist!" muttered the Bag Lady.

I was in the shed at the time.

After Mavis and Lumpy's curry in the shop I went home and decided to take a look at the shed. In truth I couldn't face sitting in the house on my own, or for that matter listening to Betty and the Bag Lady. And I had only been in the shed once - the Go Boy incident.

Perhaps I should revisit it, before I made any attempt to cut it in half.

The shed was full of finished and unfinished paintings and

sketches, loads of them all along the same frontal winds theme; surreal paintings, full of codpieces and bottoms; hard lines and dark colours in almost unrecognisable landscapes of rocks, beaches and pubs. His male figures were very Toulouse Lautrec imposed onto a Salvador Dali type landscape. He was using sand, pebbles and beer mats with acrylics. It was a whole new look for Rodger, who now used passionate, impatient brush strokes in muted purples and grey.

The pictures were a very camp take on the male nude in a surreal Scottish landscape; new to me. And I, as usual, was painfully aware of how little I knew about the man I had been with for so long.

It was all so male.

And what was worse, there was nothing of me, nothing in his art or his notebooks; nothing to show that I, his partner for ten years, existed. Not one mention apart from one newspaper cutting amongst a pile about the Argyll and its new owner breaking records of cuisines and entertainment; me being the entertainment.

It was written by the editor, who was the sort who could compliment and insult in one sentence. At the time when the article was published, I wasn't sure how to take it; was he laughing with me or at me? But I do remember that Shifty came out looking like a hero for feeding the elderly not only a free Christmas meal, but a *"five star treat worthy of a five star article"*.

From what I could recall, it was more Bisto and dairy whip than five star.

Even now after all these years, it was not an easy piece to read. The gig was all Rodger's idea, "we'll put you in a plum pudding, *inspired by the festive season*, and you can burst out of it - it will be an entrance for the gods."

And it was Shifty's idea to not only use a hospital trolley *on its last legs*, but to pour some out-of-date cherry brandy on to the pudding and light it, and I trusted them...

Sleeping Dogs Lie in the Argyll

It was Christmas Eve in the Argyll, and Shifty promised, not only 'melt in your mouth turkey, but a night of Eastern Promise', I was intrigued.

After polishing off a trifle worthy of seconds; a plum pudding the size of an out-house was dragged onto the floor and lit by Rodger; Nefertiti's partner and all round saint.

Smoke filled the room. Someone yelled for a fire extinguisher, and others headed for the door. But Ethel knew what to do, and with a pint of Tartan Special and a can of Irn Bru she took control.

The article was long, filling a whole page in the *Fyne News*, talking about, among other things me punching my way out of a *"soggy papier mâché-pudding while tossing Turkish delights from hidden crevices into the audience."*

It was not an easy article to read, especially when the writer went on to describe how my dance was interrupted, by Bingo, a dog who having never uttered a noise in years began "howling like a wolf thanks to the *"god-awful music"*, and latched on to my *"sequinned padded bra, like a leech refusing to let go…"*

It was, according to the editor, *a scene remembered by some, talked about by a few and had Bingo barking whenever the smell of brandy hit his nose.*

It was tough when that article came out. For a start I never wore a padded bra in my life, and the Turkish delights came from the plum pudding; no crevices were or ever have been involved in any of my performances. I wrote into the *Fyne News*, but they never published my letter; apparently padded bras and crevices are okay in an article but not in the complaints page. Instead they gave me some free advertising, *"Nefertiti will be performing at the Loch Fyne rest homes next Saturday week, Rodger, her manager stated that the plum pudding will remain at home."*

Rodger thought it was all a huge joke. "Relax," he said. "No one reads papers in the old folk's homes." But Rodger was wrong; in fact, many in the homes were disappointed when I entered without my Christmas pudding, and with my bra intact.

I screwed the paper into a ball and kicked it into the air like a rugby player; *at least he didn't call me a lush like some did.*

The ball knocked an ancient *naked firemen for charity* calendar from a nail, which toppled to the ground landing at my feet. Behind it dangling from the same nail, like a forgotten wedding dress in Mary's Wheels window was our codpiece.

Memories came flooding back of a time when Rodger, full of surprises, swung before me with nothing on but his codpiece

I stood in the shed, listening to Betty outside and wondered about revenge. How good it would be to get even. Sheryl seemed to think that letting go was a better choice, the Bag Lady seemed to think that it was okay to bite off less than you could chew as long as it wasn't an onion. Me, I had no idea. I looked about the shed; there was so much damage I could do, so much pain. I wanted to create pain, get even, hit something. But the artist in me could not justify the destruction of his work. After all, I told myself they were pretty disgusting; the world should be given the chance to ridicule them.

Rodger's shed also had a cupboard full of exotic nettle and dock-weed whisky. I had no idea that his homebrew had soared to such heights. Rodger's homebrew was usually strictly packet stuff, but this looked precious and it tasted delicious. And each bottle was from a different region with different names: Peat Bog Spring 1998, Crinan Canal Autumn 2001...

Betty had now made herself at home beside the Bag Lady; she was sipping tea and talking animatedly about Shifty, oblivious to her companion who appeared to have given up putting her fingers in her ears and was now meditating while singing at the same time.

"Shifty says, 'what do you expect, Zumba-ing at your age'!" said Betty. "What a thing to say to your mother. Still, nothing surprises me about him. I told him old folk are folk who get called good for their age because they remember their PIN in the post office; he laughed and said 'you don't even have a PIN'."

Betty gulped the last of her tea.

"And that," she said, "is my son's idea of a joke - my son, the reason why the coil was invented.'

The Bag Lady told her that was no way to talk about her son, but Betty didn't hear.

"I told him I needed time to get used to this new artistic arrangement and next thing, he hands me applications for sheltered housing. Me, in sheltered housing! That's when you don't need to remember what time of day it is, let alone your PIN. I am not that far gone yet. And let me tell you, I didn't spend forty years knocking up fry-ups for guests to end up in a two by four room waiting for bingo and fish and chip night!"

The Bag Lady started to hum.

"I mean, who is this 'I love my shed' Rodger?" said Betty. "What's he got that Shifty's ex hasn't?"

I downed a small glass and felt the hot liquid fill my stomach and all my worries slipped away. I picked up the codpiece (or bugle as Rodger liked to call it) and swung it about in the air.

To wear the bugle you tied it around your waist. At the front was a long swinging appendage which concertinaed in and out. At the tip was a red ball which, in the past, pulsated in time to the music. I put it on and began to swing to the memories of Hozzam Ramzy music; it felt liberating.

If only I had some music to play I could go crazy.

I experimented with deep lunges and leg kicks and the codpiece joined in, swinging underneath, enticing me to do more.

I swirled my hips as the girls kept singing, I squeezed my muscles tight and released, the codpiece plopped into a move. It felt brilliant, and I began to wonder what it would look like in the mirror. I jumped, I turned, and it followed, then I saw Rodger's iPlayer and flicked through his music... ABBA, The Beatles, Dolly Parton, *there had to be something*. And then right at the end Penguin Café Orchestra? Out of curiosity I chose a song, Gile's *Fanaby Dream* and waited.

The violins started slow, classical and I was about to turn it off, when the violins sped up enough for me to stamp my feet; more violins joined in and I wiggled my hips, and the codpiece followed, like a partner up, down and across. The more I moved the more it followed, even when I bounced on my heels.

It was like having your very own troupe on your hips!

I shimmied my shoulders, moved my chest up and down - sideways and twirled a full bodied twirl, the codpiece following like a brightly coloured streamer. It felt great.

The violins became more animated; as the double bass and drums joined in. I kicked my legs into the air, *watch that bugle fly,* followed by some lunges, *watch that bugle swing* and then I jumped up on the chair, grabbed the bugle with my hand and swung it around like a cane. I jumped off the chair, grabbed a paint brush and twirled it like a cane, *that wasn't much fun.* I dipped it in some water and flicked it at the wall, *that wasn't much fun either.*

Then as the music built to a crescendo I tossed the paint brush across the room, *that felt great.* I twirled around the shed, grabbing a cloth from one of the shelfs, tins of paint fell about the floor and I danced around them – "Who gives a fuck?" I shouted. I was dancing with Rodger's bugle.

I swung out of the door into the moonlight, around the smouldering coals of the fire. I twirled my hips, my breast to the moon. I was dancing to the trees, to Mother Nature, to the girls - *except I couldn't see them.*

I was alfresco dancing; and I didn't need a partner. As my feet pressed into the cool damp earth, as mud squelched between my toes, I swung my hips and let go of every dark feeling in my heart and the codpiece followed. The trees surrounded me like an audience in the dark, their large trunks sprouted forth from the ground like magic, and their branches goaded me to continue...

Or maybe it was just the home brew...

As the string instruments built to another crescendo I danced about the fire, swirling Rodger's paint rag around until the music stopped and Puss screeched as I stood on her tail. *Where are they? Where did everyone go?*

Puss looked at me with a 'where do you think' look. I noticed a torch light in the tee pee, and then I heard Betty's voice –"it's quite nice in here isn't it?"

Betty has no sense of smell.

Chapter Twenty-Nine

THE ART OF WINNING

What comes around has usually been around before and is way past its best.

I woke up that morning with plans. According to Deirdre McConical one can only avoid the inevitable for so long and it was now my time. I was going to throw everything to the wind, move on, and, take charge.

"Birthmarks or spots are mine for the taking," I shouted at Puss, she didn't bat a whisker.

I was going to pick up all Rodger's shed stuff, his posters, pens, beer mats, everything I could get my hands on, and sell what I could. Then take the proceeds and whatever was left to the Argyll Hotel with a witty note about negotiation. I had listened to all, now it was my turn to change things. I was after all Nefertiti, a dancer in the dark, I could play games, let Rodger think he had won. If he wanted to sell everything then I was one step ahead.

Lumpy talked about gaining and losing ground like First World War trenches, he talked about catching wasps with honey, and how beauty spots came and went. He even called me smart and adaptable and was going to say more until Mavis stopped him.

"Sometimes retreat is the only option," Lumpy said, "but you need to retreat with something on offer." And then he mentioned that word negotiate again. "That's what you need when faced with men and sticks."

Well I was facing more than men with sticks, and I knew what I wanted. Some of my happiest times in years had been by the fire with herself trying not to breathe in the stink of fish. And I was letting it slip away over what? Stuff I didn't want? I knew what I really wanted, not the slow cooker or the toothbrush holder. I didn't want revenge at all, I just wanted the Co-op Bag Lady and her collection of skulls to stay in my garden.

That morning as I rolled up the last of Rodger's shed posters and placed them in the *Rodger's half-price bin*, the Bag Lady abruptly stopped singing. I looked at my watch, it was an hour before coffee break and way too early for Betty; I wondered why she had stopped. I made us a coffee and went outside. Rodger had arrived unannounced, and on his own...

I stood at the doorway, coffee in one hand and a Snickers in the other, thinking about joining the Bag Lady in the sun, when I saw him hobbling around the corner with one crutch. The idea of Rodger coming to see me had me in a spin, it was the last thing I expected as I wasn't ready for him.

For a brief moment I felt like a girl, excited, until he appeared closer. He didn't look pleased to see me. I told myself it was his jaw clenched and wired that made him look so angry. Then I consoled myself that perhaps Rodger was not coming to see me at all. He was merely out on one of his 'stocking up on E45 cream' jaunts, and I was the last thing on his mind.

I walked back into the shop. In truth, I knew that he had come to ruin my morning. He looked as angry as his last note was vicious.

"If that goose-feeding pyromaniac touches even a hair of a paint brush," he wrote, "I am going to screw your belly dance shit up into a ball, cover it in geese crap and then set it alight. Either that," he wrote "or sell it all on eBay". *The choice was mine...*

So when I heard the Bag Lady shout, "Every shed has a silver lining," I knew the worst... I threw the last of my cappuccino down my throat and braced myself. And before I even had time to wipe the froth from my lips, my ex had filled the entrance with his six-foot frame, and was looking straight at me.

It had been a busy day in the shop. The sale on Rodger's books had gone well. It seemed that no one could resist a free pen or a 'buy one get one free' bargain, even if it was about sheds and fish. Rodger looked pissed.

Normally the Bag Lady, would be pushing the door open with her foot by now, seducing the client with her offbeat sense of humour; " come in, amigos, plenty to read"; "feast your eyes on the ancient art of womanhood", "DIY books half-price". But she didn't, she was quiet, she even stopped playing her organ.

Rodger looked at my 'help yourself' pile of shed pens and postcards and the blank walls and then noticed the posters rolled up and piled in the corner. "I was told you were having a sale of all my stuff," he said through a closed jaw. "But I didn't believe them. Neff wouldn't do a thing like that I said to Shifty - sell my things." He paused, picked up a shed pen and then looked at me, "or even worse - give it away."

"I had a plan - you interrupted," I said.

"What, to sell everything and buy a bigger tent for herself out there?" Rodger said with a wave of his cane at the Bag Lady.

I wanted to tell him about my plan, and my witty negotiating note *except I hadn't written it yet*. But Rodger was quietly angry, and there is nothing more intimidating. I watched him hobble about the shop, finally stopping at the half-price basket full of DIY books. He picked one up.

"Help yourself," I said, *trying to lighten the atmosphere.*

Rodger snorted to himself, while flipping through the book, dropping it back in the basket and picking up another one. I wondered if he was going to *flick* his way through the whole pile and thought about asking why as he had chosen them all, but thought better of it. Rodger was now breathing heavily, working on an outburst.

Rodger looked up from his book and glared. "All my things?" he snapped; *the outburst was coming* - I braced myself...

"How's your foot, Rodger?" interrupted the Bag Lady.

Rodger stopped mid-sentence and we both stared. She was like an apparition, standing in the entrance, with the morning sun beaming behind her like a halo.

The Bag Lady is rarely seen upright as she has the great skill of moving unnoticed, an impressive feat from someone in her tartan get-up. So her height always comes as surprise; she is much taller than anyone would imagine, almost six feet and very upright like an ex-dancer or someone who was once in the army. She smiled from me to Rodger and I noticed a few teeth with a flash of gold at the side of her mouth. For the first time; behind the grime and wrinkles I saw Deidre McConical and wondered why I had never noticed before?

"Good to see one crutch," she added, "now the healing has started."

Rodger muttered an uncomfortable, "thank you".

The Bag Lady asked about his jaw, and as Rodger stumbled to answer I looked at him. I wondered what Rodger was thinking, because normally after the heavy breathing he would be shouting; *not easy with a wired jaw*. Instead he looked bewildered, as the Bag Lady walked into the shop; she stood beside Rodger almost as tall as him and patted his cheek.

"Not long now," she said, "before you'll be biting into an apple again."

"Can't wait," he muttered.

"And this stick will be at the Oxfam."

"I'm keeping the stick," he said and almost smiled.

"A cane unused," said the Bag Lady "ends up leaning against walls or in cupboards getting in the way. The best thing for a cane is under the hand of someone who can't walk."

Rodger's face softened as he muttered, "maybe you're right."

Then the sun went in and the rain began. At first it was a dribble and then a downpour, followed by thunder.

I was surprised; the Bag Lady usually disappeared before the rain had even begun, before a drop had splashed on her head she was off, with her backpack full and on her back. Sometimes I didn't even notice she was gone. I would hear the rain on the window and look up from the shop bench and her space would be empty, except for a coffee mug.

Rodger limped outside and before the Bag Lady could say anything he began to pack up her camp like the end of a picnic. With his broken foot suspended, Rodger perfected a balance folding up her blanket, placing it in her rucksack and putting the organ in its bag. The Bag Lady gestured to help, but Rodger held up his hand with an *I'll do it* gesture, and then hobbled with her bags into the shop. The Bag Lady's dull tartan outfit hung loosely on her upright body as she watched, without a word.

Rodger placed her bags on the floor like a porter at the Hilton and she, like a guest at the Hilton, nodded a thank you. The funny thing was, it seemed so natural.

The Bag Lady refused a lift, but placed her bags on her back and once there was a break in the rain headed out the door. We watched as she walked upright despite the bag on her back, oblivious to the people around her.

Rodger looked about the shop uncomfortably; "she won't be able to sing here much longer," he said, "the petition is huge."

"I know," I muttered.

Rodger was quiet, not angry as he talked about Imogen's relentless form filling to get the Bag Lady into a house, at a place where no one wanted to live.

"I'm sorry," he muttered.

Rodger pulled an envelope from his pocket and handed it to me. "I thought you'd better see this before it was in the paper," he said, with a weak smile, then he made to leave and stopped at the door. "She can stay," he said, "until it is all over."

I opened the envelope after Rodger had gone, I shut the shop and sat on the couch; it was next edition of *Fyne News* opened at the "for sale" page. The house and the shop were up for sale, and on the next page was Imogen's Prance and Pose day advert.

I wondered if Mavis knew.

Chapter Thirty

NEGOTIATIONS

Shaking hands is as easy as shaking your head and much easier than shaking a leg

It was a late finish that night and the rain didn't stop, I was in the middle of cashing up when Rodger sent me a text. "When are you at the house," he asked, "I can meet you there, I need a few things."

I wondered what he wanted.

Although the rain started mid-morning in Lochgilphead, it had been raining in Ardrishaig since the night before, and the roads were now flooded; water was bubbling up from drains outside houses, cars were driving past splashing up water like small waves as people dashed into their homes. I arrived at the house the same time as Rodger; we met at the top of the drive to see water making a path for the shed.

"The drains are blocked somewhere," said Rodger, "get hold of Shifty and tell him to bring his drain rods."

I'd never seen Rodger move so fast, and with a crutch. I followed behind only to hear swearing about where the hell the water was going and then silence.

Thanks to Go Boy the shed door hung loosely from the shed, and had been tied by me with a bike lock, and the bike lock had put up little resistance to the wind and rain that had happened the night before. The shed door had been pushed free of the shed by the water, and now it was slumped on ground with a foot of water pushing it into the wall. It crashed rhythmically against the empty shed.

"Where's my fucking paintings?" said Rodger. The bag lady came out of the tee pee.

Shifty arrived reversing his Fiat with a 'what the fuck!' down the drive. We all turned to look as he parked the car on the flooded drive, jumped out of the car and skidded onto his back. It was the tarmac underneath. Thanks to our 'let's have toast, sausages and eggs on a Co-op tin foil barbeque tray' evenings there was a small patch of oily leftovers. Shifty had skidded on a portion of Chubby's sausage left out for the birds and then cursed; to quote Betty "like someone out of a *goddamn* Quentin Tarantino movie".

Betty, poking her head out of the tent, laughed loud enough for all of Ardrishaig to hear.

Rodger supressed a grin, and muttered something about treading carefully.

The tee pee was dry and safe having been built near the house and on an incline instead of the shed, at the bottom of the garden, the bottom of a decline and right near the canal.

Shifty walked into the garden, saw a bottle of home brew wedged between the shed and the door. He picked it up, looked at Betty laughing at him and made the wrong assumption. He walked over to his mother standing outside the tee pee, and asked, "why was she drinking in the afternoon".

"I haven't," said Betty, who was innocent by all accounts.

"Then why are you laughing, this isn't funny, is it?" Shifty turned to Rodger with an *I'm right* look and slipped on the bath mat, breaking the bottle of nettle whisky, which, apparently stung like nettles on his grazes from the tarmac. Shifty swore again.

By this time Betty had her mobile out and was filming, even though the Bag Lady said filming without asking was sacrilegious.

"This is YouTube gold," said Betty. "Triple viewing figures at least."

The Bag Lady did her best to warn and finally shouted "the shed".

The canal had risen and was now seeping into the lawn, while on the other side was the water from the drive - the shed was in the middle.

We watched as the shed slowly collapsed, along with my plans to make a home, Rodger's plans to take it, sell it or whatever else he had planned. Everyone stared at the remains of the shed with the out of date, firemen's calendar floating in a puddle.

"It was a stupid place to put the shed," said Betty, and no one answered. The rain had finally stopped.

The Bag Lady opened the flap of her tent. Rodger saw his work neatly stacked and undamaged. Each piece wrapped in one of his oily rags like a Christmas present and on the top, like a cherry on a cake, was the codpiece.

Chapter Thirty-One

THE RETURN OF THE PYRAMID

If you don't listen to your own inner guidance, it will stop talking.

Rodger, Shifty, Betty and I moved the paintings into Shifty's fiat while the Bag Lady held the tee pee open. It was a slick operation, completed under the duress of excessive mud, two more falls by Shifty and a "mind the bloody paintings," shout by Rodger; while Puss licked the tarmac like it was ice cream.

Later on in the week, Shifty and Rodger appeared, and Rodger and I picked up the pieces of the shed and handed them to Shifty, who tossed them like Frisbees across the garden onto a bonfire.

"That is what that deserves," he shouted, with unnecessary enthusiasm. While the Bag Lady fried fish and potatoes and stewed a pot of tea on her more sedate camp fire which now had a new home under the pyramid.

Rodger and I had made peace over a floating shed and an out-of-date calendar, it was the last thing I expected, until that is, I saw the firemen calendar hanging in the tee pee. Whether it was the Bag Lady or Betty I had no idea, but apparently, a nude fireman holding a kitten in just the right place was something they liked looking at.

That night as the sun set we all ate fish while Betty *yet again* explained how only an idiot would pitch a shed so close to the canal and on a decline. This time Shifty said nothing; Rodger had opened the last of the sloe gin and now that his ankle was almost better he had offered to drive Shifty home.

The Bag Lady told a story which had a beginning, middle, and no end; a story of an old man and his plastic barbeque apron. Which had everyone but Shifty laughing. Shifty instead stood up rubbing his knees and other sore bits, with a confused expression.

"If you wanted a barbecue," he said, "you just had to say."

EPILOGUE

Bitterness ruins even the finest features of a face like a tomato in the sun.

Six months later - the end of the beginning or the beginning of the end.

As the sun rose I looked outside my bedroom window to see herself's socks hanging on the pyramid. I watched as the Bag Lady pulled the redundant pole from the back of the garden and rammed it into the ground by her tee pee. She then pulled a slate from the newly erected shed and began to attach it to the top of the pole. I watched her spread breadcrumbs and a lump of butter onto the table and sit back as a robin jumped onto it. Puss made to jump, but the Bag Lady stopped her with a toss of conker.

I went back to bed hoping for more sleep, only to feel Puss on my bed, holding a rolled up sock in her mouth like a dead mouse. I got up, staggered downstairs; pulled apart some Tesco's chicken and gave some to Puss. She gulped it in a mouthful and joined me on the couch until the robins began to flood the table like a Disney cartoon; then Puss was off, only to be shot down again by the Bag Lady, this time with a volley of conkers.

It wasn't long after the shed incident that someone from the Social came to the house. The Bag Lady and I sat in my lounge room and offered them coffee. The Bag Lady wasn't considered homeless if she was now living with me and the tee pee was, as Imogen said, only for recreation and/or storage. The Social didn't look too hard into the tee pee, but instead gave the Bag Lady, now she had an address, a living allowance. And for the first time since I'd known her the Bag Lady didn't have to sing for a living, which is just as well because there was nowhere left for her to sing. The *Read and Be Thankful* had been sold and was now a deli with a few tables and chairs outside...

Rodger did put the house on the market for a while, but he forgot how slow the market was in Argyll, of course the Bag Lady showing people around didn't help. Finally, pleased with the sale of the shop he gave up, and instead took to visiting now and then, sometimes drawing the Bag Lady.

The Bag Lady, to the annoyance of the neighbours, started to feed stray cats, and Puss returned to sleeping on my bed and cleaning herself again. Puss spent more time inside staring out of my bedroom window; probably counting cats. But when the Bag Lady came inside Puss was there before she had even sat, rubbing the Bag Lady's leg. Betty finally accepted that the Bag Lady was not a psychic and stopped arguing about teabags. Instead they made names for stray cats and spent time in the garden, planting different herbs to make different types of tea with.

Imogen left the Social soon after the *shed incident*. Turns out Rodger's Frontal Winds exhibition hit a note for many at the Calarden and beyond. The Wee Bit of Art shop became a success, so much so, that Imogen began managing it, and even began Zumba classes in Oban.

Rodger and I in the end cleared the *Read and Be thankful* together; it was actually very easy as we both hated and liked the opposite. Rodger filled the Argyll with his shed posters and pens. While my lounge room turned into a library of self-help, goddess and cookery books. Which the goddess group of four, Sheryl, Kay Iona and Mavis, used as anything from a foot stool to a door stop, though occasionally we read them.

❄

I watched the Bag Lady picking off stuffing from the inside of the chicken and placing it on the bird table. I knew where Rodger was, Mavis had texted. He was sitting in the community centre, ordering Shifty about where to hang his paintings. I suspect that Rodger was having the time of his life.

For months I had avoided the community centre and the Wall of Gratitude. After taking my equipment from the store room, I couldn't face it. However, a few days before Rodger's Frontal Winds preview, *a one off exhibition before the closing down of the community centre for renovation,* I along with Sheryl braved the community centre.

We went along, to see how the preparations were going. Lumpy and Mavis were outside hanging up a banner. In the kitchen was the WRI organising a buffet and as we walked past the Wall of Gratitude, Imogen's portrait was hanging above the yoga and cookery teacher like a large black head waiting to be knocked of its surface.

Imogen was wearing a red outfit from God knows where. It was like a giant tartan sock coordinated in red and green, which according to Mavis was all the rage. I had my doubts.

"Knitted trousers aren't natural," said someone female, from behind me. "And as for ponchos... Who wears ponchos? Even on a size ten it looks ridiculous." And then the female began to argue with her friend about Imogen's size, finishing with a 'she must have got dressed without the lights on' comment.

Imogen had signed the photo *'Ever yours'* at the bottom in an artistic scrawl with the date and two kisses – so like her. I was about to walk on when I saw it in the background of the portrait: something familiar, white, fat and with his feathered backside in the air.

"Is that one of those geese?" I heard from behind yet again. I peered closer at the photograph. Was he doing what I thought he was doing?

Members of the WRI had now collected behind me and some were beginning to laugh. The goose had stolen the show; he was caught in the act of providing some free range manure.

"A goose doing Zumba. Who'd have thought it?" I heard someone say. Others began to laugh, mumbling things like 'do you think he's got rhythm?' 'put your right foot in, right foot out and shake it all about' etc.

I continued to look, underneath her photo was a note – but not how Imogen had *brought dance in Argyll into the twentieth century*; just a notice about the future renovations of the community centre and a rethink of the *Wall of Gratitude*.

****

Would you like to read more? Does Mavis and Lumpy tie the knot? Does the Bag Lady get a bigger tent? And if she does, does Betty sleep over? Keep on reading for a preview...

Book 3 **Four Takeaways And A Funeral** is out now at your favourite store.
Turn the page for a taster.

FOUR TAKEAWAYS AND A FUNERAL

"Love at First Dip"

Mavis and Lumpy had decided to get married, and they planned a small do with a "hot and spicy" theme, a few close friends, and a celebrant on Skype.

"We want no fuss," said Mavis. "Just lots of food, great photos, and belly dancing."

Mavis and Lumpy have been an item for about a year – and a happy Mavis has taken a bit of getting used to. While I've spent the past year on my own, struggling with blocked drains and leaking roofs, Mavis has moved in with her soulmate – a man who loves to cook, occasionally cleans, and has even been seen stocking up on massage oils at the chemist.

Lumpy has turned out to be quite a catch. Not only is he comfortable with a hammer, he cooks like a pro – his latest passion being all things hot, spicy, and foreign. He can take mincemeat, mashed potatoes, and even toasted cheese to a new level of exotic, tongue-tantalising, "what the hell is burning my mouth?" treat. Nothing, according to Mavis, passes his lips without a hint of turmeric or a dash of ginger.

And Mavis, it seemed, was happy – until the Taj Mahal reopened.

The Taj Mahal is the only Indian restaurant for miles and had been closed for years One day, with no warning, the "Closed" sign was turned to "Open," and soon there was a queue on a Friday night. The pakoras are legendary. A police shift is never complete without a bag of them, and The Roadworks Man, who has practically lived at the place since it opened, swears by their aphrodisiac qualities. *Although I have yet to see any evidence.*

Lumpy took one bite of Tenzam's pakoras and stated that they were "the dog's bollocks."

At first, the chief took offence – until he saw Lumpy's review on TripAdvisor. Lumpy talked of pakoras like they were as elusive as truffles and as succulent as fillet steak...

"His chicken is as soft as butter, coated in batter that snaps, crackles, and pops. One bite and you'll never look at a battered sausage again. As for any vegans out there, the chief will rustle up a tofu that would fool a Texan."

What a Texan had to do with tofu I have no idea, but it rubbed the chief up the right way – so much so that Lumpy began to put on weight.

"Pakoras are the way to go," he was fond of saying. But Mavis, it seems, was beginning to suffer...

She was finishing up her shift at the post office when I walked in. Normally, she would want a coffee so we could talk about her wedding plans, but this time she looked frazzled. I made a joke about spice being more than just a mouthful, expecting a smart comment back, but what I got was a glum look.

Mavis pulled out a peppermint and began to crunch. "I had no idea that pleasing a man would involve so much... indigestion." She swallowed.

I thought I saw a tear in her eye, and I asked her what was wrong.

"Lumpy knows I'm a korma woman at heart," she huffed and pulled out a tissue. "I may occasionally venture into a jalfrezi, but this whole spice thing..." She dabbed at her nose. "...it's too much! I mean, green chilli and eggs for breakfast? How can anyone face that over breakfast TV?" She blew her nose.

"I see," I said.

She slammed the till shut. "Why should Lumpy always have what he wants?"

I was taken aback. I looked at Mavis. It wasn't that long ago she was saying the opposite – "Why shouldn't he have what he wants?" – and had even made jokes what she "did" for love.

"I laugh in the face of heartburn," she'd said. Mind you, she'd been at the Bag Lady's sloe gin at the time.

I stared at her wilted face. What had changed her?

"He spends more time with that chef than me... and the chef hardly speaks English. I mean, what have they got to talk about?" She slapped some coins into a bag and tossed them into the safe. "Every time I look for Lumpy, there he is in the takeaway, chomping into something extra large and triple fried. What's that doing to his heart?"

Mavis walked to the door, pulled the sign to "Closed," and stared at me. "And they are always watching some Bollywood film full of young women, half dressed and dancing in the rain. What's that doing to *my* heart?"

Lumpy had always been partial to dancing, but I didn't have the heart to remind her.

"I never see him anymore," she muttered.

"Maybe it's wedding nerves," I said with little conviction.

"Yes, well," she snorted. "Weddings are all about compromise, and now it seems he can't even spell the word!"

Now on sale at your favourite store
Regards and cheers
Kerrie Noor

A NOTE FROM THE AUTHOR

I hope you enjoyed Nefertiti's adventures inspired by my time teaching Bellydancing. Although I have never invited a stranger to camp in my garden, the Bag lady was inspired by two strangers, a man who sang off key in front of the Co-op and another elderly drunk who shouted at me for crossing the road when a bus came hurtling by. The bus missed me by inches...
You can find me and my groovy blogs at
www.kerrienoor.com
And
like me at:

 facebook.com/kerrienoorwriter

 x.com/kezzamac

 instagram.com/kerrienoor

THANKYOU

Julia Gibb - editor and proof reader,
who went way beyond the call of duty and helped me out big time.
Marie Phillips from the WoMentoring Project,
who mentored me during the first stages of the novel; without her I
suspect this novel would still be the ramblings of my blog
For another delicious cover from:- libzyyy from 99designs.co.uk